FOLLOW THE RIVER HOME

Follow the River Home

CORRAN HARRINGTON

ARBOR FARM PRESS

Albuquerque

afp

ARBOR FARM PRESS

P.O. Box 56783, Albuquerque, New Mexico 87187

arborfarmpress.com

Printed by BookMobile, Minneapolis, Minnesota USA bookmobile.com

Distributed by Itasca Books, Minneapolis, Minnesota USA itascabooks.com

Cover design by Ann Weinstock

Interior design by Sara DeHaan

Cover photography by David Muench

Publisher's Cataloging-in-Publication

Harrington, Corran, author.
 Follow the river home / Corran Harrington.
   pages cm
 LCCN: 2015915159
 ISBN 978-0-9855200-2-1 (paperback)
 ISBN 978-0-9855200-3-8 (e-book)

 1. Vietnam War, 1961–1975—Veterans—Fiction. 2. Gay men—Fiction.
3. Post-traumatic stress disorder—Fiction. 4. Loss (Psychology)—Fiction.
5. New Mexico—Fiction. 6. Rio Grande Region (Colo.–Mexico and Tex.)—
Fiction. 7. Psychological fiction. I. Title.
 PS3608.A7816F65 2015   813'.6
               QBI15-600194

For my grandmother, Dorothy Harrington

CONTENTS

Deep, unspeakable suffering may well be called a baptism, a regeneration, the initiation into a new state.

—George Eliot, *Adam Bede*

FOLLOW THE RIVER HOME

PART ONE

The River Reader

Clouds Over the Flyway

FOR FIFTY YEARS, whenever the pull of the earth threatened to suck him feet first into some quicksand grave, he would imagine himself a sandhill crane flying above the Rio Grande. He could see forever. In early spring, the river below carried an abundant runoff reflecting cottonwoods still bare—the view in autumn a path of gold, just before the leaves went dry and fell from their mighty limbs. And though Daniel Arroyo rarely took the lead in the V-formation, and sometimes strayed from the echelon out of a failure to raise his wings at just the right time, he never completely lost the flock. Some great bird would inevitably circle him, draw him back into the formation with currents of air from below its mighty, flapping wings. And so it was that the yearly migration of the sandhill cranes became forever his escape, forever his compass.

Daniel first learned about the cranes from Helen Sedillo, when he was just eight years old. She looked up from hanging clothes on her line one Saturday morning and saw Daniel peeking over their shared fence.

"Hi, Daniel!"

He waved, smiled back. Mrs. Sedillo's voice was a song that played across the old North Valley neighborhood, her face the picture of kindness that caused all the kids to gather at her table on hot summer afternoons and drink the Cokes she kept stocked in the icebox on her porch.

Oh, she could holler at her boys for taking one more lap around the street on their bicycles, and not coming in when they were called; she could even scold Mr. Sedillo once in a while. But the anger never lasted beyond the appropriate moment, never escalated beyond the suitable level. And when adults sat in Helen's living room sipping coffee, spilling family secrets, her face revealed no judgement. Her hushed voice murmured words of understanding during late night phone calls from other grownups in the neighborhood. I hear you; I see what you mean. She dispensed advice to a parent only when asked, and wisdom gently to a child only when needed. It was in this way that Helen Sedillo became a welcome guest at all the birthday parties, baptisms, and graduations. It was how she became the neighborhood confidant, the keeper of its secrets.

"Are you going to sit on the ditch bank today? The water's only going to run for another couple weeks, you know." She put two wooden clothespins into the side of her mouth as she pulled another T-shirt out of the laundry basket and quickly glanced at the boy who was, by now, looking away. When he looked up again, Mrs. Sedillo had the same concern on her face as she had right after his baby sister's baptism. Carmen had slept in her mother's arms the entire time, even when Father Baca sprinkled the holy water on her forehead. As the family exited Sacred Heart, Daniel had pulled on his father's suit jacket and said, "We have to do it again. She was asleep!" But by then Miguel Arroyo was shaking hands with the guests. "Tell Father Baca we need to do it again," Daniel repeated. Just then he felt the solid hand of Helen Sedillo on his left shoulder. She leaned close and whispered, "It's okay, Daniel. God doesn't mind one bit when babies sleep during their baptism."

And now here he was at the fence just six months later, with Mrs. Sedillo and her same worried look. Daniel quickly lowered his head again.

"You going to the ditch?"

The ditch. That magic place he discovered as soon as he was old enough to walk around the corner. It ran only during irrigation season, March through October. It was lined with old cottonwoods, just like the one in his front yard, and you could sit on its banks and dangle your bare feet in the water that went muddy every time a bullfrog broke its surface. Box turtles slept on old wood, while blue dragonflies darted among the cattails. And the wild asparagus that grew there—Daniel's mother could always tell he had been at the ditch by the sweet smell of the wild asparagus on his jeans.

But he hadn't been to the ditch since the day Carmen died. And just as Daniel was thinking how to escape the question before it came again from over the fence, the first cranes of fall sounded in the distance. Daniel and Helen both looked to the northern sky, as the mighty trumpet call grew louder. The October sun had moved south, revealing an expanse of the deepest blue, just before the year went dark.

As the flock came into view, the cranes took turns in the lead of the cacophonous V-formation. Helen Sedillo, now standing at the fence and pointing to the sky, said, "They're heading to their winter home, Daniel. The river is like their road, only it's called a flyway."

She glanced at the boy, who still stared upward.

"If you save a place in the sky between April and November, they'll come back again in springtime."

Those words would echo across the landscape of Daniel Arroyo's life. For Daniel, the migration of the sandhills became the promise never broken, the putting to rest of old seasons, the beginning of new. Grandmothers would tell grandchildren, as they held hands during walks along the river, and pointed toward the sky. His own grandmother would soon tell him about the cranes, only in Spanish. And a few years later, when he was trying to coax Jeff Murdock's little sister out of the crawl space across the street, Daniel started to tell her the story of the sandhills.

"Do you hear that, Emily? It's the cranes. They're going home, but they'll be back. I promise. Come on, Emily, have a look."

But her gaze remained toward the ground.

"I already know about that. Grandma told me."

On this day, though, Daniel Arroyo began to see the sweeping New

Mexico sky as a great canvas resting upon an easel of cottonwoods. He could paint what he wished—a blazing sun, thunderheads in the distance, a rainbow after an August storm. Or he could paint nothing at all, and just wait for the thousands of cranes that would fill the empty space above him twice each year.

By the time three more flocks had flown over, Helen had forgotten the question that Daniel didn't want to answer. Was he going to the ditch today. It was the first time the sandhill cranes had saved him.

It had only been two months since Carmen died. For Daniel, though, she would die again and again, as his years gathered like autumn tumbleweeds along an empty road. His hands would never lose the memory of how his baby sister felt that day, as he reached into the crib to stroke her head. His arms would scream at him across the years, forbidding him to erase the memory of her weight as he held her. Daniel's hands and arms were equally unforgiving when he went to Vietnam a decade later. His fingers never forgot the slippery wetness of a buddy's blood pouring from the gaping hole in his neck. His arms never forgot the sudden drop of a comrade's head, as it snapped back the moment the soldier died.

But whenever Carmen's face appeared, or a rolling thunder could be heard in the distance, Daniel could at least remember Helen Sedillo's words from over that fence that day, and imagine himself a sandhill crane soaring just beyond the reach of gravity—a gravity of guilt that would tug at him for fifty years. When the frightened faces of those young soldiers would appear, though, the taste of choking smoke and the smell of wasted blood would pull Daniel Arroyo back to Vietnam, never letting him go home. Not even the sandhill cranes could rescue him from that.

Where Two Rivers Collide

HE IMAGINES THE tail rotor propelling to the ground at a sickening angle, still whirling, the rear gunner falling like a bullet toward the earth from the now bladeless, careening chopper. Though the scene appears in slow motion, he cannot run away fast enough as the tumbling blades cut some medic's legs off at the knees just fifteen yards away, leaving a bloody stump of a man. Daniel Arroyo drops his rifle and feels for the old pocketknife. He imagines plunging it deep into the medic's heart just to put the man out of his misery, or maybe just to stop the screaming before it becomes another unerasable sound track blasting across his sleepless nights.

Daniel is only twenty, but he might as well call himself a man, because boyhood is far behind him, lost to the acrid smoke of mortar explosions that come in the night, to screams so chilling they make you want to kill the grievously wounded buddy you played poker with just yesterday. Gone are the images of his youth—a pick-up basketball game in a backyard filled with neighbor kids, a patch of wild asparagus along a ditch bank. Gone are those who gave him comfort—his baby sister, Carmen, who smiled every time he peeked into her crib, Jeff Murdock from across the street. Every sense has been assaulted in this terrible place. The sweet smell of his grandmother's bread has been replaced by the stench of dying flesh, the song of the sandhill cranes high above the Rio Grande now drowned out by a surface-to-air missile streaking across the sky in search of its kill. The taste of tamales at Christmas has come under attack by the salt fish and peas of C rations, and too much cheap rum drunk one night in a Bangkok bar. Leeches suck at the skin on the bottom of feet that once ran barefoot on the lawn below an old cottonwood. And the feel of Jeff Murdock's powerful biceps during an impromptu wrestling match has been replaced by the touch of limp arms that now hang by bloody threads to the torso of some other lost boy—a lost boy whose unknowing family wakes to just another day in a crowded Chicago project, or maybe to a waiting harvest behind a solitary farmhouse on some Kansas prairie. Perhaps someday he will write this family, tell them he was with their boy when he died, that he comforted him by stroking his arms, his face—perhaps he will lie and say their boy was not afraid.

Daniel picks up his rifle, never even takes out the pocketknife. He dives for cover in the thick brush, waits for a half hour. The medic's screams have stopped. When he hears the sound of a patrol boat in the distance, he begins crawling toward the river, just fifty yards away. His dog tags scrape along the ground, making deadly and revealing sounds as they clink onto the small, smooth pebbles. He stops and listens. Charlie is everywhere—in the branches of every banyan tree, flat on his stomach in the rice paddy to the east, in the rocks that turn into land mines beneath your feet. Daniel flings the dog tags over his shoulder and tucks them into his shirt, where they rest quietly on his sweaty back. A leech sucks at his right ankle, and he resists the urge to jump up and pull it off.

The elephant grass to his left suddenly moves, and he aims his rifle, readies his grenade. It is only the wind, and he continues toward the river. A helicopter hovers in the distance, the sound of its blades chopping at the air, neither coming closer nor retreating. When someone radios the pilot that it is safe, he'll land in a clearing at the edge of the jungle and wait—the chopper blades still whirling like a tornado among the branches of towering palm trees, sucking dry peat toward the sky, slapping marsh grass to the ground. Two medics will pour out from the helicopter, laden with the tools of triage—tape and tourniquets, stretchers and stethoscopes. They will run from the chopper with heads ducked until they escape the vortex of the whirling blades, past torn limbs flung far from the bodies to which they once belonged, past empty eyes that now stare at nothingness. They will run in the direction of those who can still moan, those who still have the strength to scream. Those men who might have a chance are carried on stretchers to the waiting chopper, which will take off in a tilting jolt, to be replaced by another, and then another. The dead must wait.

Daniel Arroyo is now just thirty yards from the river's edge—just thirty yards from rescue, though it might as well be thirty years at the pace he is able to crawl. The jungle has gone empty of the sound of human voices, save those few who still cry out—some for their mother, others for the girlfriend they hope still waits. And some just swear through their blubbering. But all about him are the sounds that only men can make. Someone else's dog tags clink on the pebbles below a comrade crawling for the river, followed by a muffled shot that renders them silent. Nearby, fresh ammo is dropped into the magazine of someone's M-16; a bolt catch breaks the silence with a snap. Static from a headset, the sharpening of a bayonet. Was that a baby's cry? He pictures Carmen in her crib.

Daniel has to stop his slow crawl each time he hears a sound not of the jungle. Sometimes he has to wait several sickening minutes until he allows himself to get a few yards closer to the river's bank. The patrol boat is idling downstream, how far he does not know. It, too, will wait for the all clear. He smells a freshly exhaled puff from a cigarette, and stops again. His father chain-smoked Marlboros after Carmen died. No, this is probably just a Winston from some GI's rations, or it could be one of those rancid rolled smokes like the one he took out of the pocket of some dead Charlie the month before and lit up as though he hadn't cared that he had just killed some other mother's boy.

The smell of the cigarette is gone, and silence is all around him now. Daniel crawls to within a tantalizing ten yards from the river, where he will hide like a baby Moses in the reeds and wait for the patrol boat that will shepherd him away from this place. He thinks again of Carmen in her crib, but this time he remembers a spot of mud on her forehead.

Daniel doesn't know how long he waits; he has lost track of time. A helicopter hovers in the distance; the sound of a boat grows near.

As Daniel Arroyo begins to rise for his run to the water, he is startled by a twig snapping beneath his dusty knees. A lone red ant is crawling up his leg, not the leech he felt just minutes ago. He looks around and sees the old cottonwoods of his childhood moving in the breeze; the banyan trees have disappeared into a fog of thirty years. There are no towering palms in this arid place. A city fire department rescue hovercraft passes him going north at full throttle; an Albuquerque police helicopter circles in the distance. They are searching for some adventurous boy lost to the river—this river. He remembers seeing the story on the six o'clock news the night before. He has lost track of time.

Daniel looks at the sun directly overhead, then at his digital watch. It reads 11:48. But what date, what year? As he struggles with memory, the familiar face of his wife, Laura, comes into his mind's eye. She had been his high school friend, then his date at the senior prom, his girlfriend after that. They had taken a wild trip through Texas the month before he left for the army, made promises while sharing a joint, as they sped across the Pecos. ("I'll come back and take care of you," he had said, feeling gallant for the first time in his life. "I'll wait for you," she had cried, as though from a scene in a movie.) Laura Patrick. A familiar fog of confusion washes over Daniel as he tries to recall her age. She had shared his last name and his bed for thirty years, had waited for him to be ready for children, and then borne him a son and a daughter. She had worked nights in her father's liquor store while he went to college. As the fog begins to lift, Daniel slowly recalls the GI bill that led him to this place along this river, and that explains the strange gear he now carries.

"What in the world is a hydro technician?" she had asked.

"It's hydrogeological technician," he had corrected her. "I'd get to be outside and along the river, taking different measurements, testing the waters. Not always be stuck behind a desk. I think I'd really like it."

Yes, he has lost track of time.

Daniel's headset is wrapped around his neck and crackling with static from where it rests beneath the shirt that sticks to his back. A flow meter lies useless on the dry ground just ten yards from the Rio Grande, waiting to be put in the river to transmit velocity data to the headset. Daniel's hands are tight around the wader rod, which he aims like a rifle at the salt cedar moving in the summer breeze. A float has been removed from his pocket, its cork cap flung to the far reaches of the sagebrush. Sweat drips from Daniel's forehead as he looks down at sand, not mud. He smells urine, but doesn't yet feel the wetness sliding down his legs. Someone has vomited, but he doesn't yet know who. To his back, the Sandia Mountains rise majestic above the eastern horizon—not a hill lined with rice paddies. Ahead, the Rio Grande—the Mekong far behind now. Daniel Arroyo has been home for three decades, but sometimes he just doesn't know it.

From the Headwaters

THE POUNDING OF the basketball hitting the concrete ricocheted like bullets across the otherwise silent night. It pierced the dark like a shot across some bow, causing an old cottonwood to shudder in the cold, its brittle leaves to tremble in ghostly silhouette against the last of the western light. Daniel Arroyo was the only member of his family not huddled on the green velvet couch or sitting cross-legged on the oak floor in front of the fire, choosing instead to shoot baskets in the waning light of December 1, 1969. He made free throws, shots from the baseline, twisting layups. He outmaneuvered imaginary opponents, drove to the basket. He even sank a hook shot from ten feet out. He couldn't miss.

Inside, his father, Miguel, paced about the living room. He alternately closed the gap between the curtains, adjusted the damper, added another stick of kindling to the sputtering fire that sent wisps of smoke into the room. The flame finally took off in a conflagration nearly too intense for the narrow chimney he and his brothers had raised, brick by brick, two decades earlier. For the third time in ten minutes, his wife straightened the same picture—a black-and-white photo of her family taken in Colorado when she was only twelve. It was as though the straightening of it would somehow bring back those subjects long gone—her beloved parents, an older brother decked out in finest Marine dress, the faithful hound who had stepped into the frame just as the photograph was taken.

Miguel Arroyo's white-haired mother, sitting uncharacteristically rigid on the edge of the couch, pressed a worn rosary between her bent fingers. To her left were two granddaughters, both caught in that middle ground between leaving childhood and becoming young women—Anna, looking down and picking at her fingernails, Lisa fidgeting and wishing she was making out alongside the ditch with David Sedillo from next door. Joey, the youngest of the Arroyo boys, sat cross-legged on the floor and leaned into his grandmother's right knee. He wondered why Daniel wasn't made to come in and sit before the crackling radio like the rest of them since this night was, after all, about him. The only one missing, depending on whom you asked, was the oldest of Miguel and Dolores Arroyo's children, Michael. For Daniel, though, Carmen was forever missing. She was always on her side in that crib, a spot of mud on her forehead, while Michael, very much alive, wore an oil-streaked uniform with greasy rags sticking out from his back pocket and worked on F-4 Phantoms in some hangar safe in Hawaii, having had the foresight to avoid Vietnam by enlisting in the navy.

("I don't want to be stuck for four years," Daniel had said to his pleading father just a year earlier. "I'll take my chances.")

"How come you're not listening?" a familiar voice said as the gate creaked open, and Jeff Murdock appeared from around the corner of the house.

"Same reason you're not," Daniel said, as he tossed the basketball to Jeff, who took two dribbles and then missed an easy shot from the top of the key. "Besides, Dad says they're going to play it again on TV in a while. If I want, I can just watch later without the whole damn family staring at me, or feeling sorry for me, and all that crap."

"Shit!" Jeff said, as he missed another shot. "Mom's been drunk since this afternoon. She started crying and slobbering before they even started."

He was starting to lose his breath, Daniel noticed. That happened a lot when he was mad.

"And Emily is her usual weird self tonight. She keeps locking herself in the fucking bathroom. No wonder Dad works late all the time," Jeff said as he missed a shot from the baseline.

"The only one with half a brain in that damn house is Kathleen. She'll let me know when they call my birthday. I told her I was coming over here."

Daniel faked right, then went left around Jeff and drove to the basket for an easy layup.

"Shit, Danny boy! Let me warm up a little bit."

"Okay, but hurry up. It's getting too dark," Daniel said, as he handed the ball to Jeff.

It wasn't so much Jeff Murdock's words, or that he sometimes called him "Danny," as it was the sound of his voice, deep before its time. Daniel remembered the first time he noticed Jeff's voice approaching maturity. They were in junior high school, sitting next to each other on the bleachers during lunch, watching cheerleader tryouts, when Jeff punched him in the arm and said, "How old do you think you'll be when you have sex for the first time?"

The question had taken Daniel by surprise. More than that, though, Jeff's low-pitched voice when he asked his question caused Daniel to look at his profile and notice for the first time a pale shadow of fine whiskers growing along a jawline still too young to shave.

They played for several minutes without talking. Daniel didn't want to admit that his stomach practically flipped out of his mouth every time he thought he heard the front door open, even though it was just the old cottonwood groaning in the wind. And Jeff pretended he didn't feel like throwing up as he listened for the creaking of the front gate.

Jeff Murdock was practiced at pretending, which, added to his strong physique and good looks, made him the cool one. And not only in Daniel's eyes. When Jeff was ten, he deliberately pitched himself off the top limb of the Murdocks' willow tree, hollering like he was Tarzan.

He never even cried when he hit the grass, or when he saw two right elbows where only one should have been. All he said was, "Shit." And just two weeks after he got his driver's license, he rolled the Murdocks' '54 Ford into an arroyo at the base of the Sandias, with the prettiest girl in school at his side—a senior. He was grounded for that whole summer, but would pile up his sheets and bedspread and sneak out his window almost every night. Yes, Jeff Murdock was cool. No one ever knew that he pounded his fists into his pillow when he was seven, pretending to hit his mother. Or that he punched out a kid in junior high who had said, "Hey, I hear your weird sister lives in the crawl space!" No one knew he waited for Emily outside the elementary school that day and walked her home, or that he cried when he heard his father trying to get her to unlock the bathroom door that night. No one knew he rose early every morning to rinse out his mother's glass, sticky with spilled rum and Coke on the kitchen counter where she last set it.

"My grandmother is against the war," Jeff said, finally breaking the awkward silence. "Mom and Dad think she's just an old hippie. I don't really care, one way or the other, 'cause it'll be over soon."

Daniel faked a pivot to the right, then drove left around Jeff and straight to the basket.

"Dad says it's going to go on forever," replied Daniel.

"No way! You watch, it'll be over by the end of summer, and then I'm moving to California, getting the hell out of here," said Jeff, as he missed another layup.

There they were, two boys playing basketball in the near dark, talking about Vietnam as though debating who would get the furthest with their girlfriend in the backseat at the drive-in movies the following Friday, when another voice tore like a bayonet at the night from just beyond the gate.

"Jeff, you better get home. They called your number right away, and Mom's been throwing up in the kitchen sink ever since."

"Shit!"

"Hurry up, okay? I'm going to try and clean up before Dad gets home."

Jeff was right, Daniel thought. Next to him, Kathleen was the only sane one in that whole house. She could take care of herself, but with Jeff gone, who would look out for Emily?

"Later, man," said Jeff, as he tossed the ball toward the basket for one last shot, which seemed to hang forever in the suddenly charged night air. Daniel watched the ball slowly arch toward the basket. He watched as it bounced too hard off the backboard, hit the rim. It rolled halfway around and then fell unceremoniously off the side and onto the cold concrete with a muffled thud. Jeff had already turned away, didn't even see that he had missed.

Later, man. The front gate closed with a shudder, and Daniel listened to Jeff's reluctant footsteps grow farther away as he crossed the street to his house. The last sound he heard was the slamming of the Murdocks' front door. In the space of that moment, Daniel wanted to run across the street, pound on Jeff's window, and whisk him far away, to Canada—maybe Greece. Even if his own birthday was the last one called that night, he wanted to save Jeff. Now Daniel was the one who felt like puking. Or maybe like crying. He couldn't tell the difference, so he did layups for another ten minutes, until darkness finally rendered the backboard nearly invisible and cold turned his hands numb, until he could no longer avoid going back inside. He stood for a moment at the front door, basketball in hand. The old cottonwood creaked in the wind, which was now picking up speed and blowing from a different direction. He just wanted to get past his family and into the bedroom, close the door, and pretend that history hadn't just changed his entire, lousy life.

Daniel took a deep breath as he casually walked through the living room, past his pacing mother and father, his grandmother—past the averted eyes of Anna, Lisa, and Joey. Had someone peered in through the gap in the curtains, perhaps from the vantage point of the dark beneath the cottonwood, they would have seen his mother's tensed jaw, her vacant eyes staring at a crooked black-and-white photograph on the plaster wall above the bookcase. They would have seen his father alternately stoking the fire and standing at the window, his grandmother's fingers wrapped around the second bead of the first decade of a pink rosary, her lips moving in prayer ("*Dios te salve, Maria. Llena eres de gracia…*").

The voice on the radio dispassionately said, "March 17th."

As Daniel turned the corner to go down the hall to the bedroom he shared with Joey, who didn't have to worry about the date of his birth, he had two thoughts. So far, they hadn't called his birthday, February 12, and thank god the porcelain nativity scene hadn't yet been set upon the mantle, just above the wrong number of red stockings. There had been enough rotten Christmases in this house.

Daniel dribbled the basketball down the hall; no one hollered at him this night.

His life changed again a half hour later, though it would take years before he understood the magnitude of his father's knock on the door and the words, "Daniel, they called your number." What he thought was, if he got his head blown off, it better not be around the holidays, or on anyone's birthday, or in late August—when his baby sister had died. He had ruined enough of those days, and he didn't want the anniversary of his own death to make things even worse. Instead, what he muttered through the closed door was, "Okay," as the slow pace of his father's steps faded down the hall.

When Daniel finally emerged from the bedroom, his sisters and Joey were playing Yahtzee, and his mother was on the kitchen telephone, crying softly. He could never be a comfort to her, he thought, as he walked quickly by. Best if he kept out of her sight, just like he did the day Carmen died. If you couldn't make things better, then at least you could avoid making them worse.

Only his father and grandmother remained in the living room. The radio was off and they were, instead, watching Roger Mudd on the television whispering his CBS special report from Selective Service headquarters in Washington, as though somehow the delayed television broadcast would yield a different result, that somehow what they had heard live on the radio was just a rehearsal, misplaced lines in a bad play. Daniel Arroyo paused just long enough to watch a bald man pull a blue capsule from a glass bowl, twist it open like a cyanide pill, and read, "November 16th." Other lives, other living rooms.

———————

He still has the pocketknife his father gave him for his eighth birthday. The blade has gone dull with the years, the mother-of-pearl inlay chipped, the handle yellowed from an old cigarette burn made one sorry night in some Bangkok bar. You can still make out his initials, DJA, though the lacquer has long disappeared. Daniel carries it in his left front pocket during the day, sets it on the table beside his bed each night. The knife has wandered much farther than was intended. It traveled from his father's hands at his birthday party in Albuquerque's North Valley, to a wild asparagus patch along a ditch behind the house. It carved initials into an old cottonwood—later, other initials into a banyan tree in Vietnam. And then the knife slipped in and out of houses that never became homes to Daniel and Laura, too many to count. Daniel's pocketknife traveled along roads running like veins from north to south valleys, midtown to the foothills of the Sandias, and then somehow back again into his valley and a fog of years that just bled into one another.

He still remembers the day they brought his baby sister home. They had waited almost two weeks after she was born—until she could breathe better, Miguel had said. It was the middle of March, and the winds were beginning to blow the dust along the ditch. It seemed to Daniel he had waited for a year, though he knew only two seasons had passed since his mother had announced another child was on the way. He knew it was a girl; he felt it in his bones. The house was filled with anticipation as sweet as the smell of his grandmother's bread cooling on the counter. Daniel stood at the front gate, determined to be the first one to see her. When the station wagon pulled into the driveway he ran out to the passenger side, before his father could even turn off the engine, and peeked in at his tired mother who bore a tiny, blanketed bundle on her lap.

"Let me see her face!" he said, as he opened the car door for his mother. "Let me see!" She was wrapped in a soft, cotton blanket that had pink flowers.

"Just a minute, Daniel. Be patient."

He held the front door open as his father carried her down the hall to her waiting crib, a long line of bouncing brothers and sisters in tow, their grandmother bringing up the rear. His mother had already fallen into the big chair in the living room, her eyes closed, her face ashen. Daniel ran into the bedroom just as his father placed her in the crib. So many smiling faces gathered around, as Miguel Arroyo gently pulled the blanket away to reveal to the rest of his children their eagerly awaited baby sister. Michael held Joey so he could see the one who now replaced him as the youngest of the Arroyos, while Anna and Lisa stood on their toes and peeked into the crib, giggling at their new sister's twisting mouth, touching her tiny fingers. His grandmother beamed from the other side of the room, while Daniel stood at the foot of the crib and patted the baby's blanketed feet.

She seemed so tiny, he thought, as the others jockeyed for position—smaller than the other babies his parents had carried into the house before her. Tired of standing on his toes to see over the shoulders of Michael and their father, he stood back at the window while his siblings patted their sister's head, touched her face. She's going to be my baby, he thought. Michael had Lisa as his favorite, while Joey clung at Anna's dress and lit up whenever she was near. No, Carmen was his baby. He would take care of her, pat her head when she cried, someday show her the asparagus patch along the ditch behind the fence—maybe even teach her to play basketball. His baby. A wild rose was whipping in the wind and scratching against the glass; dust was flying up the ditch, still waterless for a few more weeks before the start of irrigation season.

When the others grew tired of their new sister, like a much-anticipated toy finally unwrapped on Christmas morning, and his grandmother went to help Dolores Arroyo into bed, Daniel found himself the last standing beside his father. Together they stared into the crib.

"How come she's so little?" he asked.

"She decided to come early," replied Miguel. "She'll get bigger."

"Is Mama okay?"

"She's fine, just a little tired."

"Can I wear a tie to the baptism?"

"Sure you can. Now let's leave her so she can sleep."

But Daniel didn't leave right away. As soon as his father was down the hall, he put his hand on his sister's tiny head, stared into her little face—a face that reminded him of the baby angels painted on the walls of Sacred Heart, where he and his family attended mass every week. And then he grinned and spoke innocent words that came from a place he didn't even know. "Carmen, I've been waiting so long for you." With that, he ran outside to play basketball with his brother, his best friend Jeff, and the Sedillo boys from next door.

Inside, the house went unusually quiet. Anna and Lisa went to the room they would someday share with their new sister, once she was old enough to leave the crib stationed across from their grandmother's bed. And Joey was on the kitchen floor making a mess of flour and anise, while his grandmother baked the bizcochitos promised in celebration of the homecoming of the new baby. Dolores Arroyo slept fitfully in her room across the hall, exhausted from the sixth child she had borne in just under nine years, while Miguel washed the car and cleaned out the garage.

And alone in her crib a baby girl named Carmen lay on her back, eyes open but not yet able to focus. She couldn't yet make out the heavy wood of the ceiling, only its darkness. The frame of the window was a blur, but the western light cast across her blanket was unmistakable, like the warm place inside her mother, already fading from memory. She heard a basketball hitting the concrete, the ringing of a backboard. A wild rose scratched at the window. She smelled bread and bizcochitos from somewhere in the house, and wild asparagus still lingering in the air from the one who last left the room. She had felt him rub her feet, the top of her downy head—had heard him call her by name. She didn't know it, but she put the sound of his voice and the smell of the wild asparagus in that place saved for memory—a vast expanse of emptiness just waiting to be filled. And then she slept.

Daniel did two things with his pocketknife the day before they left the North Valley house for the only vacation the family ever took—a road trip to San Diego to see the ocean and his cousins in the summer of 1959. He chiseled Carmen's initials into the old cottonwood, and then—when Michael unexpectedly appeared from around the corner and said the worst thing Daniel could have imagined that day, "She was just a baby, asshole!"—Daniel held the knife to his older brother's neck and, for just a moment, imagined Michael's jugular spraying red in every direction—past the bark of the tree and onto the wood fence, soaking into the dry earth beneath his feet, dripping down the cracked stucco on the front of the house. He pictured Michael collapsed at his feet, staring helplessly into Daniel's eyes—his final words an apology, a pleading for mercy. "I'm sorry, I didn't mean it. Please help me...."

Instead, Daniel quickly moved the pocketknife away from Michael's neck and punched his brother in the stomach. He didn't know how he got so lucky, but Michael decided not to tell their father.

Daniel spent the next morning stuffing his swim trunks, a pair of shorts, two T-shirts, his toothbrush, a Batman comic book, and his favorite model airplane into a brown grocery bag labeled DJA, which he put on the porch to join four other bags, each showing the first name of his brothers and sisters. There should have been one more bag, he thought. Where did all her things go? She was only six months old when she died, but she had things. She had a white, lacy dress she wore at her baptism. She had a pink nightgown and soft, white shirts; she had little socks and a pair of white shoes; she had diapers, and a blanket with pink flowers. Where were her things—her bottle, her bib, the baby carriage? She had a teddy bear their aunt gave her the first week she was home. It was almost as big as she was. Where did it go? Did his mother throw her things away some dark night, when she thought everyone was asleep, like she did with the cat's litter box and ball of yarn the day it jumped the fence and got hit by a car? Daniel had been awake the night the cat died, standing in the dark and staring out the living room window, as though that old cat would somehow show up on the porch, meow to come in from the cold. He watched his mother carry the litter box with the ball of yarn sitting right on top of the dirty sand, and a bag of what remained of the cat's food, and put everything in the garbage can next to the gate. Daniel saw it all; he even peeked in the garbage can the next day, and stared at the litter box for one last time. Did she throw away Carmen's things too? Should he have looked in the garbage can two days after the funeral mass, when he first noticed her things had gone missing? Too late now, he thought. There had been almost a year's worth of garbage pickups since that day. Did anyone clean that spot of mud from her forehead before they set her in that little coffin? Too late.

While everyone ran in and out of the house, rearranging and adding forgotten items to their bags—Anna her hairbrush, Michael a deck of cards, Lisa switching out one doll for another—and as his mother and grandmother packed the cooler, Daniel climbed over the fence to the ditch behind the house. Helen Sedillo waved at him from her back patio.

"Have fun on your trip!" she shouted.

As Daniel sat among the wild asparagus for one last time before they left, he heard a loud clunk from inside the yard. He peeked through the gap between the pickets only to see his father straightening the cover to the crawl space, and walking slowly away. Just before he disappeared around the corner of the house, Daniel saw his father take a handkerchief out of his pocket, wipe his eyes, and blow his nose. As soon as Daniel was sure his father wasn't going to return, he climbed back into the yard and walked over to the crawl space, its covered entrance protruding from the base of the house like a grave. Daniel didn't see anything unusual on the ground near the opening, and there wasn't enough time to lift the lid and check it out. He had been in there only once, when he was six and Miguel had let him crawl around while he checked for a leak in the pipes. It was dark and dusty, and full of bent nails and bits of copper wire that his father had told him to watch out for. There were chunks of broken concrete in the dirt and spiderwebs hanging from the support beams. In the distance Daniel thought he could make out the furnace—its pilot light glowing like the first star at dusk. But there was no getting into the crawl space today. Maybe when they got back from their vacation, he thought, he and Jeff Murdock could go down there when his father was at work, and his mother was napping, when no one else was around. Maybe they could sneak down a couple of Cokes, blow out the pilot light, and see how long it took for anyone to notice. For now, though, Daniel just headed for the cottonwood.

"What are you doing up there? I thought you guys were leaving today!"

Jeff's voice rang out from near the top of the Murdocks' willow tree, and crossed over the street to the old cottonwood where Daniel now perched. From his vantage he could see Jeff waving from the tree, then giving him the finger, which the boys had learned how to do just that summer. Daniel laughed for the first time that day, while Kathleen and Emily ran through the sprinklers in the untrimmed lawn below their brother, who was now laughing hysterically from the top branch of the willow. The Murdocks' garage door was open, revealing a mess of rakes and shovels and cluttered workbenches, but no car. Those kids were so lucky, Daniel thought. Mr. and Mrs. Murdock let them stay alone all the time.

"We're leaving in a little bit!" hollered Daniel. "Anna and Lisa are taking forever to pack!"

"You're lucky you'll be seeing the ocean! Pee in it, or bring me a seashell or something!"

Daniel laughed again, until he looked down and saw his father's dis-approving glance.

"I'll give you a quarter if you say you peed in the ocean at the first show-and-tell. Mrs. Johnson will have a heart attack!"

"Daniel, get out of the tree!" Miguel said.

Mrs. Johnson. The last person Daniel wanted to die was Mrs. Johnson. The coming September would be the second time he started third grade in her classroom, only this time Jeff would be there. Two bad things had happened the year before. Jeff Murdock had flunked second grade, making it impossible for him and Daniel to be in the same class again. And Carmen had died. Daniel figured he couldn't do anything about Carmen, but he could use her death as an excuse for flunking third grade without getting into too much trouble, and end up in Jeff's class again. And nice Mrs. Johnson had been the key. He sure wasn't going to get off to a bad start by shocking her classroom with a story of peeing in the ocean.

"See you when we get back!" said Daniel.

What he really wanted to tell Jeff, though, was to sneak into the back of the station wagon and hide beneath the brown grocery bags and his parents' suitcase, to duck behind the cooler or crawl under the red and blue bedspread his grandmother had knitted as a gift for his aunt and uncle. What he really wanted was to haul Jeff out to California with them. Or, better yet, to ask Miguel if he could stay behind—he'd mow the lawn, take care of the house. There would be more room for everyone in the car. He'd promise to stay out of the cottonwood, the elm trees. After all, the Murdocks let their kids stay alone and nothing bad ever happened; surely Daniel was old enough, too. He was almost nine and a half. Instead, he slowly climbed down from the cottonwood and went around to the basketball court to get in a few last shots while Miguel finished packing the car.

He didn't hear his father calling him the first time, or telling him to use the bathroom before they left. He didn't hear the others piling into the station wagon, the doors slamming shut, the cacophony that was their excited voices emanating from the rolled-down windows. He never heard the screen door slam, or his father say, "Where the hell is he?"

"Daniel, get in the car!" Miguel shouted for a second time, now visible from the corner of the house.

"Put the basketball in the shed and get out here!"

Daniel reluctantly got into the station wagon, the last one in. He sat by the passenger side window behind his mother, with Anna and Joey crammed between him and Michael, not unlike how his grandmother sat pressed between Miguel and Dolores in the front seat. Lisa was in the back with all the luggage, having pulled the shortest straw in the contest the night before to see who got to ride in the back first. She had won the right to stay there until Gallup, three hours away, when it would be Michael's turn.

"Lock your door," Dolores Arroyo turned and said.

Everyone in the car went silent for just a moment, as Miguel put it in reverse. They were leaving Carmen behind—the blue Chevy station wagon as full with people as it was with silence, scraping bottom as it slowly backed out of the driveway bearing one less child than it should have. Where would she have sat in this crowded car? On his lap, he thought. He would have wrapped his arms around her, held extra tight when the road became bumpy, kept her safe.

The excited voices and laughter of his brothers and sisters resumed by the time the car was in drive. Jeff had already gone inside, but Daniel waved just in case he was looking out his bedroom window. That's when he saw Emily. She was in the Murdocks' garage, emptying a can of red paint all over herself and the garage floor. Daniel waved again, this time at her, as the station wagon rounded the corner. She didn't seem to notice.

The gnarled cottonwood was the last to see them go.

———

He spoke of Carmen only three times as a boy, and one of those times didn't count. When he was ten years old he blurted out something to his grandmother, who couldn't understand his English (he never intended to try it in Spanish). She just hugged him and kissed his head, and then wiped the tears from his face with the tissue she kept folded in her sleeve. Daniel's brown eyes and dark wavy hair, the dimples above the soft jaw line, reminded her of Miguel when he was her boy. So many times she had told him he looked just like his father ("*Parece como a tu papá,*" she would say with a smile).

"*Qué pasa, mijo?*" she said softly, as she handed him a chocolate chip cookie. "*Habla me en español.*"

"*No importa,*" Daniel replied, slowly chewing the cookie and wiping the crumbs from the corner of his mouth.

She stared at him for a moment, and Daniel was suddenly afraid she would ask him again and that he would have to make up something, as the urge for the telling had passed. So he finished wiping his eyes and put on his biggest grin. His grandmother pinched the dimples she loved so much, and then he ran outside to the basketball court before she had a chance to ask him again what was wrong, to say it in Spanish.

The second time Daniel spoke of Carmen didn't really count. He was eleven and on his knees in the confessional at Sacred Heart on a Saturday afternoon, hands clasped in supplication and muttering to the robed figure sitting in the dark on the other side of the veiled screen. He hadn't planned to say anything about his baby sister, as he stood in line with all the others and made a mental checklist of his various offenses of the preceding week.

"Bless me, Father, for I have sinned," said Daniel as he made the sign of the cross. "It has been one week since my last confession," he went on.

He could never remember if the priest was supposed to say anything at this point. So, after a pause, Daniel went on.

"I hit my brother on the way home from school, I cussed twice, and I broke a lamp and told my mom it wasn't me."

The usual silence at this point always caused Daniel to feel a little sick in his stomach.

"Is that all?" the deep voice from the other side of the screen finally said.

Is that all. No, thought Daniel, that was not all. And suddenly he whispered, "I think I did something to my sister a really long time ago."

Daniel didn't wait to see if Father Baca had heard him. Instead, he got up and bolted from the confessional, didn't even genuflect on his way out, or dip his fingers into the holy water just outside the sanctuary. The red light above the confessional door went green, and the next person walked in, no doubt confused by a follow-up question, or some penance meant for a young boy's ears. Daniel was by then running across the parking lot as fast as he could.

The third time he spoke of Carmen was to Jeff Murdock, five years after her death. It was a blazing July afternoon, and they were in the asparagus patch along the ditch behind the house, smoking a Kent cigarette Jeff had stolen out of Dorothy Murdock's purse. Daniel never remembered how it was they ended up there, though he was certain it was Jeff's idea.

"It'll just be an experiment," Jeff said, as he tossed the cigarette butt into the ditch. "It doesn't mean anything. I mean, we need to know what we're doing when the time comes."

When the time comes. Daniel knew Jeff was thinking about that blonde girl he had been hanging out with since Easter break—leave it to Jeff to get a girl two years older than he was and whose parents both worked. Jeff could spend long afternoons at her house, after telling his parents he was going to the movies with Daniel; or weekend nights, saying he was camping out in a tent in the backyard with the Sedillo boys. Jeff used his bedroom window to come and go more than he used his own front door.

When the time comes. A fire broke out in the pit of Daniel's stomach, and he wanted to hold his best friend on top of him, to look him in the eye and stroke the triceps that grew stronger with every day, to run his fingers through Jeff Murdock's thick, brown hair, to slip his hands beneath the back of Jeff's T-shirt, then just slightly below his loosened belt. He wanted to kiss him and then to feel Jeff's rapid breaths upon his neck, and in his ear.

But there was to be no kissing, as they were in junior high and each already knew how to do that. And this was just an experiment, he thought, as Jeff hung his belt over the Sedillos' fence. Instead, Daniel just said okay, as he unzipped his jeans, pulled down his pants, and turned over on the ditch bank.

When Jeff was done, he lay for a brief moment on Daniel's back, and Daniel wished they had removed their shirts so he could feel Jeff's sweat. He wished Jeff would stay there longer, give him a soft kiss on his shoulder, maybe whisper some nice words in his left ear. But Jeff didn't linger. Instead, he rolled over and said, "Okay, your turn. But hurry up, so we can shoot a few hoops before dinner."

And so it was that an asparagus patch along a ditch bank was where Daniel Arroyo first made love. And it was where Jeff Murdock had sex for the first time, though he would always say his first time was three years later with the blonde girl in the backseat of the Murdocks' '54 Ford on some empty dirt road in the Sandia foothills.

When they were finished, and pants were zipped and shirts tucked in, Daniel leaned into Jeff and said, "You remember the day Carmen died?"

"Yeah."

"I think it was my fault."

Running the Rapids

Daniel woke six minutes into the last leg of the Continental flight heading for Albuquerque, as though from a nap on a lazy summer day. There had been a jolt, and now his fellow passengers were screaming and crying and praying. He did not join them. Instead, he rubbed his eyes and blinked a few times, thought of the conference he had just attended in Newark. He even yawned as he glanced across the aisle and through the far window at the flames of the exploded engine streaking across the Texas night sky. Daniel Arroyo was the picture of calm. Not even the sensation of tumbling out of control and being sucked toward an unforgiving gravity caused the smallest surge of adrenaline to course through his blood. There was no panic, no pounding heart. His mind was clear, empty of the clutter of sentimental flashbacks to childhood, or visions of dead ones with whom he surely would soon be reunited. Some might say he was numb. He even stared out the now upside-down window, as though the stars below were no more than the fading lights of Houston, casually loosened his tie, and undid the top button of his maroon shirt.

This was a familiar calm, first experienced in an unlikely place. There had been another explosion in another time, where fellow travelers screamed in panic, where human limbs hung from banyan trees like branches broken in an August typhoon. A bloody platoon sergeant who seconds earlier had pushed Private Arroyo into a trench had screamed at him, "You fucking idiot!" These, the words he managed to spit through the blood pouring out of his mouth where front teeth used to be. And all Daniel could think was how odd a man's last sentence could be. "You fucking idiot!"

Daniel had been napping in the soft sea grass of the Mekong Delta and had not heard the order to stay low. When he rose to pee, all hell broke loose. A lone Vietcong guerrilla was hiding in the brush with a grenade. When Daniel stood, Charlie emerged from the marsh with a crazy look on his face. He fumbled with the pin, then managed to toss the grenade in Daniel's direction, but not before Sergeant Taylor shoved Daniel into the trench. The grenade exploded, ripping apart Charlie along with the platoon sergeant and three of Daniel's comrades. "You fucking idiot!" Sergeant Taylor had yelled at Daniel, the femur of the sergeant's right leg barely holding on to the rest of his thigh. "I was going home!" he screamed, as blood poured from the left side of his jaw and dripped out of his left ear. "You fucking idiot!" And Daniel, in shock and nearly paralyzed by fear, could only zip his pants and wipe the urine off his boot.

But the platoon sergeant's final words had eventually pierced his illusion of calm, and Daniel looked around to see again the jungle at the edge of Vinh Long and the familiar faces of his platoon members—at least, those who survived. The three dead comrades were unrecognizable, of course, save Wayne Thorp from some suburb west of Detroit, whose severed head still bore the kind of expression he might have had after losing a hand of poker. Nothing more than an inconsequential disappointment, when the stakes were so low as to not matter. There would be no last words, no final thoughts from Wayne Thorp. It had all happened too suddenly.

But this was a different night in a different place—a Continental jet streaking through the Texas sky. It was not until some young man shouted, "It's okay, he's got it under control!" that Daniel felt a slight sickness in his stomach at what had just happened. They were headed back to Houston, the pilot announced to the passengers, now silent except for a terrified woman still whimpering to someone on the opposite end of a cell phone that was never supposed to have been turned on. What words had she chosen for her last, he wondered. None had come to him. In the fear and numbness, there was little sorrow for a life about to end, or for anyone below who might be left to grieve. Laura was tiring of him; he could feel it. There had been too many screams in the middle of too many nightmares; too many twisted sheets; too much sweat on the pillow. She couldn't even muster the disappointment for him their daughter felt, or the disdain of their son. Molly felt so sorry for her father she could hardly look at him across the dining room table, and she just wanted to save her money and move to California. She would miss him, he supposed, at least a little. But Jacob, who now patrolled the ruined roads of Baghdad in army specialist insignia, was doing all he could to not turn out like his father. There were no final words.

Daniel had already fallen asleep when the sound of the exploding engine had jolted him back to consciousness. He saw the river of flame through the window across the aisle, but all he could think of was the conference he had attended that week in Newark, and how the chemicals he found performing tracer tests along the Rio Grande paled in comparison to what floated just below the surface of waters greater—the East River, the Hudson. Then, as the plane tipped backward, his brain skipped to two scientists from Los Alamos lab, swept away a few years earlier in Mortandad Canyon, drowned in rain and mud and a radioactive soup that flew off the fire-stripped canyon walls and rushed through the normally dry channel. Did they have time for any last thoughts, he wondered? Did they hear the waters rushing toward them? That could have been him in that canyon, but his company had lost the contract for the well-monitoring.

The screams had come mostly from the other side of the aisle, the side where the engine had exploded. And they were mostly the screams of women, until a booming male voice yelled a single word, "No!" Would that be the man's last utterance? Daniel wondered. Just one ineffective word, one impotent final order? It was at least fifteen seconds before the passengers on his side of the aisle stopped staring in confusion at the commotion on the other side, and joined in the panic that had by then overtaken even the seasoned flight attendant in the jump seat behind him. Daniel turned around and looked over his seat. A lesbian couple across the aisle and one row back were holding each other close and saying their goodbyes. Daniel couldn't save any of them.

A middle-aged married couple sat next to him. They seemed to have chosen silence as their final statement, as they held hands tightly and spoke not a word. But then the woman suddenly shifted in her seat and let go of her bewildered husband. She grabbed Daniel's knee, then clung to his shoulder, his neck. She plastered her head against his chest, drove her polished fingernails into his maroon shirt. The greatest sorrow he had ever seen, Daniel thought, washed over her husband's face as he watched his wife reach not for him, but for the stranger at her side. Would there be any last words, or would the woman's husband just leave the world with a feeling of resignation, even jealousy? And as for Daniel, should he put his arm around the wife, give her the comfort her husband would have readily bestowed? Should he reach across her and put his hand on the man's trembling shoulder? After all, it wasn't as though they were drunken strangers dancing in some darkened bar, Daniel having cut in before the jukebox went silent. They were about to die together.

And what of the last words or final thoughts of all those others gone before? Did his father think of anything in his last moments, or did the morphine drip coursing like a river through his veins render him not only speechless, but without thought? And where, then, in the weary, cancer-ridden body does memory hide? Surely Miguel Arroyo remembered that August afternoon he ran down the hall with his baby girl in his arms, mud on her forehead. Surely he remembered how he flew out the front door and handed Carmen off to Helen Sedillo, as he started the old station wagon and pulled out of the driveway with a lurch that nearly stalled the engine. Or perhaps death was kinder and gave Miguel the grace of recalling a different day, a day in spring when he carried that baby girl in the opposite direction—from the arms of Dolores sitting in the station wagon, through the front door and down the hall, for all her waiting brothers and sisters to see.

And what of Jeff Murdock, who never saw his twenty-first birthday? Did he think of that summer afternoon along a quiet ditch where two boys lost their virginity not on a double date with girlfriends, but behind a wild asparagus patch with each other? Did he remember he had hung his belt over the Sedillos' fence and almost left it there? Did Jeff Murdock think of Daniel as he lay dying in the mud along the Mekong? Did he imagine its waters running not toward the South China Sea, but through a ditch to the Rio Grande? Not likely. He probably thought of his little sister, Emily—pictured her wearing mismatched clothing that didn't fit, and a thick layer of red lipstick that bled from the corners of her mouth. He probably wondered who would watch out for her. Or maybe death was more generous and gave Jeff a picture of himself crawling out his bedroom window some summer night, off to meet a new girlfriend. Maybe he had the sensation of flying, as though from the willow tree in the Murdocks' front yard, only this time he never landed, never broke his arm.

The stuff of final words, final moments. And what could a baby girl named Carmen have ever thought? Daniel was, after all, the last person she saw. Did she recognize his voice, or the smell of their grandmother's beans on his breath? Did she ever smell that wild asparagus, or feel the wetness of the mud on her forehead? Did she hear the basketball bouncing against the rim, or the scratching of the wild rose on her window? Did she remember Daniel's smile, or wish that he had come back in, checked on her one more time?

It was well after midnight when the second plane landed in Albuquerque, carrying only a third of its previous passengers. The cab driver never said a word, not even when Daniel handed him a generous tip in the darkened driveway. Laura had turned off the light hours earlier.

————————

The house went cold and silent over the next two months, save the occasional conversations about the road trip Daniel and Laura were planning. It was really Daniel's plan. He figured she wanted to leave him, and who could blame her? Too many nightmares, too many ghosts—dead babies and shredded young men—had shared their bedroom on too many nights. Maybe he and Laura could go away, Daniel had suggested. Recreate that trip they took across Texas the summer before he went to Vietnam, only this time wearing clothes and leaving the marijuana behind.

But you can never take the same trip twice, especially using an old map. Roads have been widened, signs changed, exits added. If there was any doubt before, Daniel was certain Laura seriously considered leaving him as they sat breathless on an empty dirt road in west Texas, five hours past where I-10 crosses the Rio Grande. Nanci Griffith was singing "Love at the Five and Dime" above the sound of the still running engine. Daniel's sweat was falling down the side of his face; his eyes were still wild with old demons. Tears were splashing off Laura's cheeks, and she could barely see. All they shared at that instant were the aftereffects from a sudden release of too much adrenaline, and the erratic rhythms of their rapid, gasping breaths. There were no words, just thirty-five years fading into a Texas whirlwind in the passenger side mirror.

Only moments earlier, Laura had screamed at him to stop, pull over, take the exit. Her voice was hoarse, as though she had cried out across the decades, across the thousands of miles and tens of years all the way to some sweltering jungle southwest of Saigon.

"Put down the gun! Daniel, please...."

His wife had been at his side through decades of a war he had only spent thirteen months in, always waiting for him to finally come home. But she could no longer live in that damn jungle, not in that sticky delta. Not any more, and Daniel knew it. After all, how many times had she pulled him out of the marsh, grabbed his ankles, dragged him through the mud of the Mekong? How many times had she picked imaginary leeches from his legs, his arms, or cupped her hands over his ears in the middle of terrible nights, muffling explosions heard only by him? The vase of red roses he had delivered for their twenty-third anniversary turned into a foaming sea of blood on a headless neck, right there in the middle of the old oak dining table as they ate his favorite dinner by candlelight. The hot-water tank went empty on a regular basis, as he tried to wash away some putrid stink only he could smell.

And their son, now breathing dust in the desert at the edge of Baghdad, had felt fatherless since high school. Jacob had been a proud member of the Junior ROTC at Albuquerque High, until a three-gun salute at the award ceremony drove his father whimpering and into a fetal position on the ground beneath the bleachers, rendering him a puddle of shame that Jacob would never again mop up. "You fucking wimp," Jacob thought but did not say. "You're not the only guy who ever went to Vietnam, you know. Get over it." Instead, when one of the thankfully few classmates who had witnessed Daniel running for the bleachers asked if he was okay, Jacob just said, "He went through a lot in Vietnam, and once in a while loud noises make him think he's still there. It never lasts too long, though."

Meanwhile, Daniel and Laura's daughter, Molly, now floating from one minimum wage job to another with nothing but a GED, certain she'll make enough to move to Los Angeles and get into the movie industry, had stayed away from the house as much as she could unless she knew Daniel was in the field, measuring some river, testing some waters. Her father could make her laugh, and he was usually fine, she thought. But his flashbacks were too unpredictable and eventually just made her too sad. She'd finally had enough one day after she tossed a tennis ball for the dog. Daniel had come around the side of the house, seen the still rolling ball, and screamed, "Grenade!" as he dove into the hedge. She cried herself to sleep for the last time that night.

And now here they were, just he and Laura, parked on some lonely dirt road, the engine still running. At least the dead armadillos were along the highway, and not here, Laura thought. At least there was nothing else dead along that highway. She reached over and put the minivan in park, turned off the key, put it safely in her pocket. The .357 Magnum was still cradled in Daniel's limp hand. She gently took it, unloaded the bullets, and closed the glove compartment. Laura got out of the van, threw the bullets as far as she could, and then walked around to the driver's side window.

"Daniel, you need to get out," she said softly, as a familiar look of confusion washed over his face. "I'm driving; we need to get out of here."

"What happened?" he said, his eyes now focused on this day, on this place. Daniel stared into the distance of the barren Texas landscape, saw sagebrush, switchgrass. Gone was the rice paddy, the elephant grass. "What happened?"

"You blacked out in the middle of the highway going eighty miles an hour, that's what happened," she said, trying to stifle an old anger rising in her as they exchanged seats. "Don't you even remember that red car?"

"No," he whispered.

"Everything was fine, and then this red convertible passed us. You caught up with them and started riding their tail. I told you to just pass them. You don't remember?"

Daniel's eyes filled with tears, which he wiped away before they spilled onto his face.

"They even pulled over to let you pass on the right. That's when you grabbed at the glove compartment and pulled out the gun. I screamed at you, Daniel."

Daniel lowered his head and then looked out the window as the tears rolled down his cheeks, and silence filled the space between them.

"I'm sorry," he said. "Are they okay?"

"Yes, thank God. You never even had your finger on the trigger. They pulled into the center divide and stopped. You came out of it right before the next exit."

Laura tucked the now empty gun beneath the driver's seat, turned the car around, and drove toward the on-ramp.

"Why are we going this way?" Daniel said.

"We're going home, Daniel."

They rode in silence, spoke not even a word as they passed a red convertible in the center divide, parked slightly lower than the roadbed, a Korean man standing outside and looking at the left front tire, his wife still sitting in the passenger seat and shaking her head. They never saw the minivan with Laura Arroyo at the wheel go speeding past in the opposite direction.

———————

Daniel spun the old pocketknife in circles atop the bar on Taos' main drag, and the instant before it came to rest, he gave it another spin. Laura hadn't yet kicked him out, but she must surely be relieved he was working in the field for this week, Daniel thought, as he gave the knife another spin. He had done this through three beers, and the pocketknife had never stopped moving, not even when he finished a frothy mug, looked up, and ordered another. To his right, an empty bar stool. Next to that a woman, her bent head and the silver hair falling over her face showing a tired kind of drunkenness. He was aware that she occasionally swept the left side of her hair out of her eyes, looked askance at him. A table of middle-aged women, most sporting turquoise squash blossoms and big diamond rings, were guzzling margaritas and hollering and laughing about husbands back in Dallas who were no doubt paying for this expensive week of museums and shopping. Laura, now in her middle years, could never be like them. Daniel looked away, took another sip of beer. The vacationing women laughed louder, as one spilled her drink. Carmen would be around their age, too, thought

Daniel. She would be approaching the middle years she never attained. Would she be sitting in some bar? Not likely, Daniel thought. No, his sweet Carmen would be in his grandmother's kitchen, making bread, serving it to her own family. Always in that old house, the cottonwood forever watching over her, the mud gone from her forehead.

Daniel gave the pocketknife another spin. A tall, lean man in jeans and a blue work shirt sat alone at a corner table to Daniel's left, sipping a glass of red wine. He was probably close to seventy. Perhaps the older woman two seats down was looking at him and not at Daniel. It didn't matter.

Some affected musician was singing a Jackson Browne song and smiling at the table of adoring Texas women, one of whom kept sending him beers. The musician sat with them during his second break. He had thick, brown hair and looked to be in his late thirties, at least a decade younger than any of the women at the table. His left sleeve kept coming unrolled, and he kept folding it back up to reveal a strong forearm that one of the women placed her hand upon. The musician laughed at all their jokes.

It was a quiet Tuesday night in Taos, save the table of women from Dallas. Daniel paid his tab, tossed a dollar into the musician's jar on the small stage in front of the monitor, and walked into the empty street to make his way back to his hotel room. He would be there for the entire week, assigned to do multiple stream gauging surveys on the Rio Grande, from the upper gorge north of Taos to the rapids south near Pilar.

The next day, after he measured the flow rates below the Rio Grande Gorge Bridge, Daniel trudged the six hundred feet back to the top, hauling the pygmy and readout meters, his headset in his backpack. He walked onto the bridge and looked down upon osprey, falcons, and the rushing waters. Is this what it feels like when you die, he wondered, as he peered over the edge. When your body finally lets go of your soul, do you just float away—above some river, then up canyon walls, past great falcon nests? Do you pause for a moment on some bridge and look at where you've been? Maybe Jeff Murdock's spirit rose high above the Mekong, above the marsh and the jungle, above the blood on the banyans. Maybe he paused on a bridge not yet blown and saw below him a place that was green with life, flowing with holy water. Did the world below pull at him like a magnet, beg him to fly off that bridge, and swim toward home? Or was that just Emily who called out his name, pleaded for him not to leave her like that? "Who will take care of me?" she would have screamed. Did Jeff soar high enough to see the willow tree in the Murdocks' front lawn? He died just sixty miles north of where Daniel had been on patrol, as close as a drive from Albuquerque to Santa Fe. Just one hour away, though the letter from Daniel's mother telling him didn't arrive for another four weeks. Did the helicopter bearing Jeff Murdock's ruined body fly over Vinh Long while his childhood friend played a hand of poker? Did Daniel, for some reason, glance skyward before placing his next bet?

As he headed back to his truck, Daniel passed the woman who sat two bar stools away from him the previous night, her silver hair still covering her face, now wearing sunglasses and carrying a tripod over her shoulder, a 35 mm camera slung around her bent neck. She showed no signs of recognition as she walked slowly past him. When Daniel reached the east end where his truck was parked, he looked back and saw that the woman had set up her tripod, the camera now wearing an enormous zoom lens. She was shooting photos of the canyon walls. Just then he spotted the tall, older man from the corner table of the bar, standing in the middle of the bridge, maybe fifty yards from the photographer. He still wore jeans and a blue work shirt. At that very moment the woman pointed the camera toward the unaware man, took his picture, then quickly swung the camera back upriver.

She returned to her car, which was parked next to Daniel's truck, and sat there until the old man went to the opposite end of the bridge, got into his car, and headed west. Daniel noticed she had removed her sunglasses and was crying, as she started her engine and proceeded slowly across the bridge in the same direction. A photographer in pursuit of a most compelling subject, no doubt. Maybe the old man is a famous Taos artist, or a great writer. Perhaps he used to be in the movies. Maybe the photography shoot was all staged, and he only pretended to be unaware of the camera, of the silver-haired photographer. Or maybe he is her lost love and doesn't know she is following him. Would Laura have ever done the same, followed Daniel onto some unknown bridge, taken his photo just before he crossed over? He wondered.

For the next two days Daniel worked the Rio Grande south to Pilar. He found the rapids of the Taos Box to have a similar magnetic pull as the Gorge Bridge. What is it about a sliver of water six hundred feet below that beckons you to jump from a lonely bridge; what is in the allure of a wild river that invites you to dive in from the water's edge, to baptize yourself in unforgiving waters? In either case you are swept over great boulders, pulled under swirling eddies. In either case you are eventually dumped unceremoniously into the sea, unless your contorted body is caught up on a broken tree limb, or stuck between a rock and the muddy bank.

Daniel returned to the Taos bar on Friday night. There was no music, just the hum of a country and western radio station at low volume in the background. The table of Texas women sat empty, and people spoke in hushed tones. A black cowboy hat sat atop the stool where the handsome musician sat just a few nights earlier, a solitary, unplugged microphone in front. A cardboard placard read, "RIP Jeremy Jones— We Will Miss You."

"What happened?" Daniel asked the bartender.

"Poor sucker offed himself; jumped from the bridge Wednesday night. They found him crumpled like a dirty napkin on the banks at the bottom of the gorge yesterday morning, didn't even make it into the river."

A week later, Daniel found himself sitting in another bar, not in Taos but on Central Avenue in the heart of downtown Albuquerque. There was no older woman balanced precariously on her bar stool; the tables had never known the likes of a group of Texas housewives on a long shopping weekend away from their husbands. There was no live musician, just pulsing bass tones coming from speakers high up on the walls. The flashing lights, mostly purples and greens and blues, flitted across the faces of two men as they shot pool in the darkest corner. Three middle-aged men sat together at the bar, talking with the much younger bartender. A man in a suit sat alone at a table, glancing at his watch, tapping nervous fingers on a half-empty bourbon. A few tables away, two other men were laughing and clinking wine glasses in unheard toasts. Mostly, though, the place was empty, as it was only five o'clock.

Daniel chose the last stool at the bar, as far from the three men as he could get, though their glances penetrated him. He did not look back, he returned no smiles. Instead, he ordered a Guinness, as the bar began to fill with men spilling out of banks and offices after long days of work.

"You look like you could use a friend."

The voice came from behind his left shoulder, deep and calm, as a second beer appeared before him. Daniel turned his head to see a handsome man about his age take a seat at the stool next to his. As the man hung his suit jacket over the back of the stool, Daniel noticed he was of average height, slender, with skin dark like his grandmother's, and hair straight and silver, features sharp. His hands were strong, Daniel thought, as the handsome stranger loosened his tie. At this point Daniel could have stood, paid his tab and walked away, pretending he really didn't know what kind of bar he had walked into. At this point he could have gotten in his truck and driven home to Laura, who had for some reason not kicked him out, not even after the incident in Texas. She was likely wondering what was keeping him so late this evening. Perhaps he could have even stopped for flowers along the way.

"Got anything against lawyers?" the stranger smiled.

"Doug!" the young bartender said, "Where've you been?"

The lawyer and bartender exchanged greetings, and then the stranger named Doug ordered two shots of tequila, one of which he placed on the bar in front of Daniel.

"Doug Mondragon," he said with a smile, as the two shook hands.

"Daniel," said Daniel Arroyo.

"You forgot to remove your wedding ring, Daniel. That will get you nowhere in here." Doug laughed.

 Halfway through a third Guinness, Daniel removed his wedding band, with only a small pang when he quickly thought of Laura.

They left just after dark.

Doug turned the key and opened the door to reveal a living room filled with miniature replicas of great statues, walls covered with art as foreign to Daniel as the acrylic bistro table Doug now led him to. A half-melted candle sat in the middle. Doug lit it, and then disappeared into the kitchen as Daniel adjusted his posture in the chrome-legged chair. This was a two-story house, and Daniel wondered just what would be said that would cause them to leave this room and climb the stairs. Whatever it was, it would have to come from Doug Mondragon.

"How about some wine?" Doug said, as he returned from the kitchen with an open bottle of red.

Daniel refused the offer of a line of coke. It was the only time he felt uncomfortable that night. And, while Doug put away the straw, Daniel couldn't help but notice the cocaine remained on the table like artificial sweetener that missed its mark.

The two men sipped merlot and talked about their jobs. Doug complained a little too much about being a lawyer, Daniel thought, but he sure seemed to enjoy the money.

"How long have you been married?" Doug finally asked.

Daniel coughed and immediately clipped his wine glass on the edge of the bistro table.

Doug laughed. "Let's go upstairs."

That was it. Let's go upstairs.

Doug was leading the way, pulling Daniel along behind him. They passed an octagonal mirror near the foot of the stairs into which neither man looked.

Daniel did not think of Jeff Murdock as he lay on Doug Mondragon's bed. There was nothing in the white leather headboard, or in the tapestries draping the walls, that caused him to think of a wild asparagus patch along an old ditch, or of two thirteen-year-old boys. The music emanating from the speakers atop the dressers sounded nothing like a basketball pounding on a concrete pad. And this was no rehearsal.

Daniel did not think of Jeff Murdock until an hour later, when Doug casually handed him a business card at the front door and said, "We should get together again sometime, have lunch or something." The words sounded strangely like an invitation to play a little basketball before dinner. Daniel pictured Jeff. As the two men shook hands, tears welled up in Daniel's eyes.

"Hey, I didn't mean anything by that," Doug Mondragon said. "Turn the card over. It says to call anytime; I really mean that. Just don't expect me to marry you."

They both laughed, though by then Daniel was thinking not of Jeff Murdock, but of a faithful wife at home.

As Daniel fumbled with his keys in the truck door, a voice rang out from Doug's door.

"Hey, don't forget to put your wedding ring back on!"

―――――――――

Daniel left Laura in the middle of the night as she slept, just two weeks later. He had woken for the third time from a fitful sleep just before 3:00. Laura's breathing was deep and steady, even when he rose from their bed and stood at the doorway. She never even moved. Daniel walked slowly down the hall to the study and quietly closed the door. The card had said to call anytime, and though Daniel knew those words had likely been written on other business cards that were now tucked away in other men's desks, or hidden in drawers beneath other men's socks, he needed comfort, or maybe he just needed a way out. He couldn't tell the difference.

The voice on the other end of the phone was deep and inviting, and that was all it took for Daniel to walk back into the bedroom, slip on some clothes in the dark, quietly brush his teeth, and shave by the light from the streetlamp reflected in the mirror. Laura's breathing remained steady, though she had at some point rolled over from her back to her side, facing away from the door. Daniel looked back once, and then stepped into the hall. He left a note on the counter saying he was sorry, that he was okay, and that he would call in a few days.

Into the Sluice

Daniel only saw Doug Mondragon for five weeks, but that didn't matter to his son, Jacob. It didn't matter that he never fell in love with Doug, or that the two men soon realized they were not meant for each other. It didn't matter to Jacob that Daniel had quickly found his own place after he left Laura. It didn't matter that he never went back to that bar.

"I can't believe you left Mom in the middle of the fucking night," the son in the army uniform, too old to reprimand for his bad language, said through clenched teeth across the table at Denny's.

"Hey, that's between me and your mother," Daniel said, though it clearly no longer was. Why the hell did Laura have to tell Jake the goddamn details? Jesus, he thought.

"I can't believe you left her a fucking note on the counter. You never had any balls."

"Cut the crap, Jake. It's not your business."

"The hell it isn't," Jacob muttered.

"You want to talk to me, then talk to me. But show a little respect," Daniel said sternly.

Jacob had been home for a month before starting a third deployment in Iraq, and agreed to meet his father only a day before he was to fly out again. Daniel assumed Laura probably had talked him into it. In spite of having put up with years of Daniel's PTSD, culminating on that road in west Texas, and his leaving unannounced for a strange man met in a bar one lonely night, Laura still cared for him, though he didn't know why. Perhaps it was their friendship going back to high school days, the senior prom. Perhaps it was just because she had taken her marriage vows more seriously than he had.

Whatever the reason, there he was with his soldier son, who stared at his father across a table of contempt.

"So, are you really queer?"

"I don't know."

"Great, you don't know. That's just great, Dad."

Daniel stared into his coffee mug and slowly rotated it around on the table, while Jacob's eyes darted from one side of the room to the other. Jacob squirmed in his chair and tapped on his knee the way he had always done since he was a boy.

"More coffee?" the waitress said, as she filled the mugs without waiting for the answer.

"Jake, I've struggled with this since I was younger than you. But I want you to know I was always faithful to your mother."

"Yeah, right, until you weren't."

The sarcasm dripped onto the table and splashed to the floor.

"Not your business," Daniel repeated. "You don't have the facts to judge me or anyone else."

The waitress slapped the ticket down. "I'm clocking out, guys, just take your time."

"I don't know the answer to your question, Jake. All I can tell you is that I have struggled with this for most of my life, and then one night everything just got out of hand after a few beers. I only saw the guy a few more times, and there's been no one since."

He didn't mention a best friend from childhood, named Jeff.

"Why did you have to go into that bar? Couldn't you have had a beer somewhere else, like the rest of us?"

Daniel went silent, stared at the floor.

"Did all this come up after Vietnam?" Jacob asked in a slightly calmer tone, his teeth no longer clenched.

Daniel looked at the ceiling, then around the coffee shop, took a deep breath—the kind that precedes the truth—and replied, "No." The only possible excuse in his son's view now gone, Daniel went on, "I had a feeling in junior high."

"Jesus, you dated Mom since high school," Jacob said as he rose from his chair and put his cap on.

"Sit down," Daniel said to his son's back as he walked away.

But Jacob would not sit with his father again until he'd spent another year in the brutal streets of Baghdad.

Ash and bone. That is all Daniel Arroyo could think of—ash and bone. He sat in the sixth row from the front of McMurphey's Funeral Home, glancing at his watch. It read 1:17. It was the same watch he had glanced at in the middle of the night he left Laura. Only then it was resting on a nightstand attached to an Italian platform bed with a white leather headboard, and it was almost dawn.

Ash and bone. An organist had played "Morning Has Broken." Doug Mondragon's mother wore a dark blue dress. There were a brother and a sister and other relatives, none of whom Daniel had met. Lawyers filled the rows behind him, lined the back wall from where an errant cell phone could occasionally be heard. But Daniel sat among a cast of men, most much younger than Doug, a couple his own age, none older. Some wore bright colors, others had donned suits pulled from the far reaches of closets. A young man sat at the end of the row, weeping, all in black, Prada sunglasses perched on the top of his head. But, as different as they each were, this row of men was a row of equals. They had each known the flesh of Doug Mondragon, his sweat, the powerful beat of his heart, his baritone voice. ("You look like you could use a friend.")

Yes, they each knew that part of Doug. Before another part drank so much vodka one night that he drowned everything but the sorrow and anger hidden behind his smile, and then ripped open the dam gates and set his blood free in a rushing cascade down the stairs and into his living room. Did Doug not know he could have called just about any person in this room? Did he leave himself any time for a second thought? Did he just for a moment think of running down those stairs, maybe getting there ahead of his blood and in enough time to grab some empty wine glasses from the bistro table, capture the red liquid before it hit the living room floor? Or was it just wasted wine to him? Did Doug Mondragon lie on a cold autopsy table and from some far-away place try to scream out, "Put my blood back in there, sew me up!" Did he feel the heat just before he was turned into ash and bone; did he wish he could emerge like some genie from the urn now perched upon a small, cloth-draped pedestal at the top of the center aisle? Could he see from just three feet away his angry mother, hear his weeping father? Did he know he was to be given to the river, his ashes baptized in her muddy water? Daniel wiped the sweat from his forehead, tried to catch his breath, focus on the minister's words.

"You okay, Dad?" the deep voice said from the other end of the phone the next evening.

"Jake!" said Daniel. "Where are you?"

"At Mom's. Well, she supposedly still lives here," he said sarcastically. "She's got some jerk boyfriend and she's hardly ever around."

"I know, I've seen them together. Jeez, what a prize," Daniel laughed. "So, what's up?"

"I'm home again, this time for good, maybe. You going to be around tonight?"

"Sure, come on over. You remember how to get here?"

"Yeah. I'll be there in about an hour."

Daniel almost didn't recognize his son without the usual contempt in his voice. He hadn't heard that softer tone probably since Jacob was ten years old. He quickly cleaned up the place, made sure there were some cold beers in the refrigerator, and put on a fresh shirt.

"Mom told me that guy killed himself. You okay?"

"Yeah, I'm fine. I really hadn't even talked to him in a long time, but I saw it in the paper and decided to go to the funeral yesterday. I'm fine. So, you're home?"

"Well, at least for a little while. I'm trying to get some things worked out, and then hopefully I'll get assigned stateside, maybe doing some security training, whatever."

Gone was the army uniform, replaced by jeans and a Lobos sweatshirt, an old pair of basketball shoes. He looked thinner, Daniel thought, younger. Jacob drummed his fingers on his knees like he had done as a nervous boy before a Little League game; he cleared his throat endlessly between gulps not of soda, but beer.

"Which way is the bathroom?" he asked his father.

When Jacob returned to the couch he was met by a fresh beer and a half-empty bag of Doritos.

"So, what are you trying to get worked out?" Daniel asked.

The pause was uncharacteristically long, the sadness in his son's diverted eyes as foreign as a street in Baghdad.

"I was on my third tour over there, Dad. I guess I sort of finally got it about what can happen to a guy's head after seeing all that stuff. I did okay the first couple of years."

"What changed then?" Daniel asked, steeling himself for the answer.

"I kind of lost it after two guys were blown to bits by an IED in the road in front of me. I just couldn't get it out of my head, and then I couldn't sleep."

Daniel took a deep breath and wiped the sweat beginning to break out on his forehead. His boy needed him for probably the first time in over a decade, and this was no time to get lost in one of his own nightmares. This was Jacob's war, not his.

"You'll be able to sleep again," Daniel said.

"No, you don't get it. I started fucking up my squad because of it."

"What do you mean?"

"I couldn't concentrate, and I blew protocol three times leading patrols. Jesus, I could have killed my own guys."

Killed my own guys. Daniel Arroyo knew that one all too well. Once he had seen a scared buddy shoot into the moving brush, only to find some GI dead in there, his pants still pulled down around his ankles. Another time the men in his platoon had to scatter like roaches when the lights come on, as an air force machine gunner mistakenly strafed the road they were patrolling. Hit by a line of explosions and fire, three soldiers never stood up. And three families back home later received letters from their boys' platoon leader, describing their bravery under enemy fire, and accepted their posthumous Purple Hearts.

"But you didn't kill your own guys, Jake. Bad shit happens in every war. Mistakes are made all the time."

"I know, but I still shouldn't have fucked up. Anyway, here I am. I've got two weeks at home before I report to the VA and some counselor. If it goes okay, I get to stay in and hopefully get back to work, maybe security training somewhere in the Southwest—not so far from home."

He shifted in his seat, knocked into his beer, and watched the amber puddle spill from the table to the floor.

Jake's eyes then turned to his father, as Daniel moved to the couch and carefully put his arm around his boy.

"You'll be okay, Jake."

This time Jake's eyes were filled with tears that fell off his chin and joined the cascade of spilled beer, like the Tigris falling into the Euphrates. Tears that Daniel Arroyo had not seen since the young man next to him was a boy who had just crashed his bike.

"How the hell would you know? You never got over it."

"Sure I did. Well, maybe you never really get over it, but you can learn to live with it. Besides, you're different from me—you're strong and courageous, and there's a lot more help out there now for you guys. You'll be fine."

In the silence, Daniel's stomach boiled as he flashed on stories of homeless Iraq vets at the mercy of unforgiving streets.

"You'll be okay, Jake," Daniel said again, trying to convince them both.

"I don't feel so brave anymore," Jacob said softly, his head still bent toward the floor of his father's living room.

"Sure you are. You'll get through this, and then later you'll be able to help someone else." Daniel wondered whom he had helped in all these years, and was glad his son didn't ask.

After a pause, Jacob wiped his eyes on the Lobos sweatshirt, sat up straight and said, "I'm not like you, you know. I have a girlfriend and I'm going to get married someday and have kids."

Daniel resisted the urge to remind his son that he had done exactly that. Instead, he moved back to his chair and said, "Let's have another beer, and you can tell me about this security job you're going to get."

Jacob ended up spending the night on his father's couch. Daniel put a blanket over him, and a pillow under his head. He watched his boy fall into a fitful sleep and wished he could wash the blood from his nightmares, erase the sound track of screams. Blood from IEDs is as red as that from grenades. Blood is blood. Daniel fought the urge to move Jacob from his side to his back, to check his forehead for a spot of mud. And then he went into the other room and called Laura to let her know everything was okay.

"He's really struggling," she said. "His nightmares are as bad as yours were. He's asking all sorts of questions about you and your side of the family, like he's trying to find enough differences to assure himself he'll be okay. I told him you never got over feeling guilty about your sister's death when you were a kid, and he wondered if that was half your problem—that maybe that's why you never got over the bad dreams, and all that."

"No way were any of my bad dreams about Carmen," he lied.

"Well, I don't know if he's more worried about bad dreams or turning out gay," Laura said. She was seldom sarcastic, so Daniel let it pass. He figured she was entitled now and then.

"He's not gay," Daniel said, stopping short of adding, "Hell, I still don't even know if I am."

"But he's definitely volatile like you," Laura said.

"I haven't been that way in a long time, Laura. You didn't tell him about what happened in Texas, did you?"

"No, Daniel. I never told anyone," she said in a tired voice.

Crossing the Dam

STILL WATERS RUN deep. That is what people would say of Daniel Arroyo. His third-grade teacher said it the day he went outside to recess and failed to hear the bell, failed to return to his class. He had walked the perimeter of the playground, eyes focused on the worn path, for how many laps he did not know. All he knew was that he suddenly looked up, perhaps because of the silence that surrounded him, and realized he was the only boy left on the playground. The monkey bars were empty, the seats of the swing set gone still, the tetherball barely moving in the March breeze. His shoes were scuffed and covered in spring dust. Daniel made his way back to his classroom undetected, until he had to open the door that thankfully was at the rear of the room where his desk was. Mrs. Johnson looked up from the story she was reading aloud to his classmates and gave him a private smile. On his way to the lunchroom, she asked if he was okay. He nodded yes. No one else said a word.

Still waters run deep. Even Helen Sedillo had said it once, not long after the experiment with Jeff. Still waters run deep. He had no idea what it meant.

Daniel heard those words again when he was fifteen years old. He was wiping the counter at his first summer job at the Dairy Queen on Fourth Street. A beautiful, older woman came in nearly every Friday for a small milkshake, vanilla. She had to be at least twenty-five, he thought. Her eyes were kind, her smile generous and meant for him. Whenever he saw her at the counter, his stomach knotted, his face flushed. He couldn't look her in the eye. But she noticed his nametag and one August afternoon said in the softest voice he had ever heard, "Daniel, don't you ever talk?" He looked up and into green eyes that sent a burst of warmth coursing through his veins and, speechless, returned her smile before averting his eyes back toward the floor. "Well, still waters run deep," she said with a wink, as she walked away with her vanilla milkshake.

"*Mi chico tranquilo*," his grandmother said, as she patted his head the day he graduated from Valley High School. "*Vaya con Dios, mi tranquilidad*," she whispered in his ear less than a year later through tears, as he left for the army.

Still waters run deep. Daniel Arroyo never heard those words uttered in Vietnam. Not of him, not of anyone else. But he heard them again many times after his return. A drunken woman perched two seats down from him at a Taos cantina, her head hung toward the half-empty gin and tonic, the vacant seat between them a bridge too dangerous to cross. Still waters run deep. His wife the year before he left her. A handsome lawyer as another beer appeared before him. "You look like you could use a friend."

But one mid-September morning, Daniel's focus was not on deep waters but on the shallows of Elephant Butte as the sun rose across the lake. He launched from the marina, then idled while he gathered water samples from the middle of the reservoir between Rattlesnake and Horse Islands, before heading for the shallows of McRae Canyon, where he landed. An orange marker he had placed the year before, where the water had met the sand, was now dry and covered in dust. The lake had receded another forty yards. He waded in, measuring the depth every three meters and recording it in his field book, until he stood nearly

waist deep. As he reached into his tool bag to exchange the depth measuring stick for a tracer test vial, a dark movement flirted at the edge of
his peripheral vision. He looked in the direction of old Fort McRae, its
adobe foundations showing through the low water just below the bluffs
of Champagne Hills, and thought he saw a woman with long, black
hair. The darkness seemed to move again, and now he clearly saw an
arm raised high, a hand moving side to side in the growing light. He
squinted, struggling to see what he finally realized was in fact a woman
slouched upon one of the exposed adobe walls. She looked as though
she was sitting on water.

As Daniel approached and cut the power to the outboard motor, he
noticed the woman was naked. As he drew closer, he could hear her
moans, see her tears. She was limp and covered in bruises and cuts. She
was sitting upright now, trying to cover her breasts, swiveling around
as he made his approach, her back to him covered in welts and quaking
in tremulous shivers. He grabbed a tarp and tossed it at her as the boat
bobbed up against the exposed foundation upon which she sat. She
fumbled with it and finally succeeded in covering herself as she turned
to face him—a frightened teenaged girl.

"What are you doing here?" he asked incredulously.

She didn't reply.

"*Como se llama?*" he said in a softer tone.

After a pause she said softly, "Carmen. *Mi nombre es* Carmen Rodriguez Bustillos."

"*Como?*" Daniel said, even though he had clearly heard her name and
was already thinking of his baby sister asleep in her crib.

"Carmen Rodriguez Bustillos," she said again, her voice growing
louder, the pitch higher.

She then launched into a flurry of words, all in Spanish and only
a few of which Daniel understood. For a moment he thought of his
grandmother, gone for three decades now, and wished she could be
there to better understand this young woman, to better comfort her
with the kind of words he no longer knew. Instead, he motioned for her

to get in the small boat, but she seemed frozen. He reached out his hand and spoke gently, "It's okay, *está bien*. I won't hurt you." She finally took his hand, crawled over the side of the boat, and collapsed into a fetal position on the bottom, her head resting on his left boot. He adjusted the tarp to cover her rear, turned the boat toward the marina on the other side of the lake, and accelerated.

This is someone's little sister, he thought. Some brother is looking for her, trying to bring her home to worried parents. Perhaps this brother stands atop the bluffs, sweeps the lake with binoculars. Perhaps he knocks on every trailer door, peeks in every tent. Yes, this is someone's little sister. Not his, not Jeff's—some other boy's sister.

The last Daniel saw of Carmen Rodriguez Bustillos was as the paramedics rolled her stretcher into the back of the ambulance. She was covered in blankets, and the blue surrounding her mouth was returning to pink. If she wasn't so scared, he thought, she surely would have given him a smile. What he never knew was that just a month later, she would say her first rosary for him from the church in the plaza of Villa Ahumada, just eighty miles south of Juarez. She would do this every day for the rest of her life.

The television news that night told of the recovery of a kidnapped Mexican prostitute, of rumors of other missing girls before her. Carmen. Her name was Carmen.

He dreamed of Carmen that night in his room, alternately waking to the blinking light from the motel sign flashing red and yellow and green across the ceiling, then dreaming again. The Carmen in his dreams was not a tortured girl from Mexico, though, but his own baby sister, lost on a steamy August afternoon in 1958.

She wasn't covered in bruises, but in a cotton blanket that had pink flowers. His Carmen wasn't naked in the shallows of a lake once deep, but at rest on her side in a crib. There were no scratches, no blood, though a missed spot of mud had been left to dry on her forehead. He hadn't yet known that his Carmen was beyond moaning, that there would be no more tears. But she was cold, he had heard his mother scream. And he saw the blue of her face as his father ran past him, the baby limp in his arms. He hadn't known what any of it meant. The last he had seen of her, she was in the lap of Mrs. Sedillo from next door, who sat in the passenger seat of the Chevy station wagon as it lurched backward out of the driveway.

Daniel was only eight then, but he still believed it could have been different, if only he had known to wake his mother. He had stood twice at her crib earlier that afternoon, while his mother napped across the hall.

"Don't bother Carmen," his mother had said. "...be quiet so I can get some sleep."

No, Daniel had never known to wake her. And he would wonder for a lifetime if, had he known, he would have dared wake Dolores Arroyo from her much needed rest.

That summer night, in 1958, Daniel had hid for as long as he could in the asparagus patch on the ditch behind the backyard fence, and had wiped his eyes and nose all over his shirt. The house had been filled with aunts and uncles and cousins, and no one would miss him as long as they were all there. At some point the outdoor light had gone on, and he heard his brother Michael start up an unusually quiet basketball game.

But he had also heard the murmur of adults talking quietly in his neighbor's yard. He listened at the fence and tried to identify the voices. It was Helen Sedillo from next door, who had held Carmen in the station wagon on the way to the hospital. He could also hear Mr. Sedillo, and Jeff's mother, Dorothy, from across the street, maybe even Marge Burns from next door to the Murdocks, though she was rarely friendly with the neighbors.

"I think she suffocated," he had heard Helen Sedillo say.

Daniel didn't know the word, but he knew it was bad.

———————

The week after he finished his work at Elephant Butte, Daniel went to visit his mother, as he did every Sunday since her heart grew too old and tired to care for itself. The door to Dolores Arroyo's bedroom, the last room at the back of her daughter Anna's house, was cracked open about five inches. As Daniel looked in on his frail and gray mother, he thought she looked like his own grandmother in her last days in the back bedroom of his parents' house. The years had reduced Dolores to a motionless mass of flesh untethered from bone, had made her eyes more vacant even than in the months after Carmen had died. She was on her back, safely between the railings of the rented hospital bed, only partially covered by a wrinkled nightgown and a pink, cotton blanket. Her eyelids twitched and her mouth was agape, revealing a small drop of drool at the right corner, about to make its way toward her chin. A blue rosary was wrapped around her left hand, the sixth bead of the first decade stuck between her fingers as though that was where she had stopped her prayers.

As Daniel took a seat next to her and cleared his throat, Dolores' eyes partially opened. Gone was the deep brown, replaced by a spotty hazel.

"Michael," she said with a half smile.

"No, it's Daniel," he said.

"Oh, yes... Daniel. Where is your uniform?"

"I don't have it any more, Mom."

"Are you home for good yet?" she whispered.

"Yeah, I'm home for good now."

Daniel wondered how his mother reconciled his silver hair and the lines across his forehead with her momentary failure to recall that he had come home from Vietnam all those decades ago. What cruelty, he thought, kept a mother from remembering her son had returned from war alive? Did she lie awake at night and picture him bleeding out in some jungle, or falling to his death from a careening helicopter? Did she hear her son call out for his mother? Did her heart pound nearly out of her chest every time the doorbell rang, thinking some army chaplain was on the other side?

"Where's Laura?" she said, closer to real time.

He lied and said she was at home. No need at this late stage to remind her they had divorced. She never asked about the kids, but he told her anyway.

"Jake is a corporal in the army now. He's head of security training at Fort Bragg. Still trying to get stationed closer to home. And Molly just moved to Huntington Beach, a nicer place than before. The baby is due in a couple months. Can you believe it; I'm going to be a grandfather, an *abuelo*. It's a girl. They aren't saying what they're naming her yet."

Daniel sat with his mother for several more minutes, holding her gnarled hand and wondering what was left of her thoughts, her memories, as she closed her eyes and went silent.

But just as he was about to leave, her eyes opened wide and she whispered, "Where's the baby?"

Where's the baby. Dolores Arroyo's voice was barely audible, her body nearly unable to move. But Daniel could still not look at his mother without seeing her rolling in agony on the grass below the cottonwood, or hearing her screams that pierced his young heart and rendered silent an entire neighborhood that late August afternoon, 1958. Where's the baby.

It could have been any number of babies she was referring to, from her baby girl who never saw her first birthday, to fourteen grandchildren who were starting to have babies of their own. Perhaps she was thinking about his own unborn granddaughter. Daniel ignored the question and, instead, put his hand on her forehead until she drifted off to sleep, or to wherever one drifts when breaths are numbered.

"I better get going, Mom," he whispered a few minutes later to the limp body on the other side of the hospital bed sidebars.

Daniel gave his sleeping mother a kiss on the cheek, but just as he reached the doorway, a stronger, more familiar voice called out from the bed.

"Dorothy Murdock was drunk. She called for help and then threw up when I got there. I needed to clean her up before Fred got home," her voice trailed off. "And Emily had locked herself in the bathroom and we had to get her out."

Her baby? Had she been talking about her baby? Maybe, but it was all jumbled up with Dorothy Murdock and Emily from across the street in the old neighborhood, and made no sense.

Daniel returned to the wooden chair beside his mother's bed.

"She was only two, and I had to get her out of that bathroom," Dolores whispered.

Clearly, this was no longer about Carmen; this was about Jeff Murdock's little sister. Daniel didn't have the heart to tell his mother where Emily Murdock lived now, that she had no bathroom, that she crouched in the salt cedar along the river when she had to go. He didn't have the heart to tell her that Emily curled up behind downtown dumpsters during the winter months, and tried to stay warm with every scrap of cloth she could find. Daniel couldn't tell his mother that Emily would have been better off still stuck in that bathroom in the house across the street.

Through the Oxbow

Daniel had heard the rumors for years, first from Marty Sedillo during halftime at a Lobos basketball game, later from one of Marge Burns' sons in line at the grocery store. Emily Murdock, Jeff's youngest sister, was one of those crazy, homeless people living in the bosque. River rats, they called them.

Daniel had not seen Emily since running into her at a gas station in the early nineties, but he would have recognized her blue eyes anywhere. They were just like Jeff's. Daniel was taking a break at one of the tables at Tingley Beach, when he noticed what appeared to be a very old woman feeding the ducks. Her skin was brown and weathered, and she had long, silver hair. She was dressed in a Lobos sweatshirt with an orange scarf wrapped around her neck. The denim skirt she wore was loose, and so long on her short frame that it nearly touched the mismatched, worn sneakers upon her sockless feet.

Just as he was about to finish his coffee and head back into the bosque, the woman approached him and asked not for money but for a black ballpoint pen. That's when he saw her eyes.

"Emily Murdock?" he asked.

She looked so ancient, Daniel thought, though she was only in her mid-fifties.

"Oh my, no, I've had at least three last names since that one," she replied with a smile that showed two gaps where pretty white teeth used to be.

"Do you remember me? I'm Daniel Arroyo. I used to live across the street from you when we were kids."

She stared for a moment, then a look of recognition crossed her face as she said, "You're Jeff's friend."

"That's right, Emily."

"You know," she said, "the last time I saw Mother it was at the post office, and Jeff still hadn't come home from Vietnam. Or maybe that was Kathleen who said that. I don't remember now. Anyway, my neighbor Phil has been back from the war for years, and he says if Jeff isn't home by now, he isn't coming home, period. End of story. Why he wouldn't come back I'll never know, because all he did was gripe about going there in the first place."

Daniel didn't have the heart to tell her Jeff had come home in a flag-draped coffin in the fall of 1970, that a rosary and mass was said at Sacred Heart, that she had sat in the front pew with her parents, Dorothy and Fred, her sister, Kathleen, and her grandmother from Corrales. He didn't have the heart to tell her she had thrown up at the gravesite, that her grandmother had wiped her face clean with a tissue hidden in her sleeve, and held her hand, or that her mother, Dorothy, had wept into the folded flag and practically had to be carried away when it was time to go. Besides, Daniel hadn't been there. Every vivid detail was written in his own mother's perfect handwriting in a letter he received in Vietnam four weeks after the fact, a letter he keeps folded in its original envelope and tucked away in his dresser drawer, behind the socks.

"You live in there?" Daniel asked, tilting his chin toward the bosque.

"Well, it's my summer home. I spend the winter months downtown," she said, as she tied her shoe.

"Don't you get lonely, or scared in there?"

"Oh, no. The neighbors are very nice. We have barbeques and cocktails all the time. Charles has a propane stove, and he watches my place when I'm running errands."

"Will you show me your place?" Daniel asked.

"Well, it's a little dirty, maybe another time. Mother would kill me if she saw it," Emily said with a laugh.

Dorothy Murdock had died a couple years before, of course, and Daniel was almost envious of Emily's ability to forget that essential fact, and of her refusal to remember her brother was long dead. What other terrible moments had she tossed off, as though discarding a used paperback when the plot became unbearable? Was there a heap of old stories hidden beneath some cottonwood in the bosque? Did she rip up the pages she didn't like and throw them into the river? Did the muddy water cause the ink to bleed to the edges, render the words unreadable?

Emily now stared at him through squinted eyes.

"Do you get enough to eat?" he said, looking at the denim skirt that hung so loose it nearly touched the ground.

"Oh, sure. Leo rides his bike along the trail, up and down all day long, up and down. He brings the appetizers—french fries usually. And Bob picks up the fresh fish for the barbeque."

"What about in the winter?"

"Did I mention the fire?" Emily said, looking toward the sky. "They blamed it on Phil, you know. But it was the boys on the bicycles. Phil just reads his Bible."

"Where do you stay in the winter, or when it rains? Do you stay with the same people?"

"I spend more time alone when I'm downtown. I get tired from all the work, and don't get out much once I leave the office," she said, as she brushed a hand across her hair.

"What work?" Daniel asked.

"The dissertation. It's almost done."

Emily Murdock's blue eyes began to dart wildly, the same way Jeff's did just before he did something crazy, like dive out of the willow tree, or back his parents' car into the middle of the street when he was only twelve.

"Well, I really must go now," she said. "I'm meeting a date at Café Benoit. We were supposed to meet last week, or maybe it was the week before...," she said as her voice trailed off.

Daniel smiled at Jeff Murdock's little sister.

"Well then," he said, "you better go get ready."

"I met him in the *Alibi* personals. This time I'm sure it's the real thing," she said with a wink, as she turned and disappeared into the bosque.

———————

Two weeks later Daniel came across another woman with Jeff Murdock's blue eyes. But unlike Emily's, these blue eyes matched a face that was instantly familiar to Daniel. He had seen them many times over the years—in the parking lot at Home Depot, at a summer zoo concert, walking along a ditch. Unlike Emily's eyes, which wandered from her feet to the sky, these blue eyes looked directly at you. They belonged to Kathleen Murdock, Emily's sister.

Daniel was only ten years old the first time he noticed Kathleen's eyes were just like Jeff's. He was at the new football stadium to see John Kennedy, when he spotted her.

"Hey, I thought you guys were for Nixon!" Daniel had hollered at Kathleen, who sat two rows down at University Stadium that crisp fall morning, 1960.

"Just our parents. They took us out of school to go see him, even Jeff. I'm voting with Grandma!" Kathleen said, as she leaned into the silver-haired woman at her side.

Daniel sat with Michael and his father. Sure, they were there to see Kennedy, but also to see the brand new football stadium. He wished Jeff had come. Emily wasn't there either, but she was so seldom anywhere. Probably locked herself in the bathroom again, or smeared her mother's lipstick all over her face.

"Where's Jeff?" Daniel had asked, as he moved into the aisle next to Kathleen.

"I don't know, I spent the night at Grandma's. I think he has to mow the lawn today."

That was when he first noticed her eyes were like Jeff's.

Now, five decades later, and coming toward him on the Corrales clear ditch was Kathleen Murdock, a grandmother herself. She stopped about thirty yards short of him and pointed toward the sky, leaning over a three-year-old grandson. Just then Daniel Arroyo heard the sand-hill cranes flying south down the Rio Grande. As he got closer, he heard her say, "They're following the river to their winter home—if you save a place in the sky, they'll return again in springtime." Daniel flashed on Helen Sedillo and the day she had told him the same thing over the fence when he was only eight years old.

But Kathleen could just as well have been describing the seasonal waters of the irrigation ditches. In fact, if not for the rusted headgate, padlocked and chained, Daniel wouldn't have even seen her that day. He was at that particular spot to meet Joe Castillo, the latest in a long line of Castillo mayordomos, who was going to loosen the gate and cut the lock so Daniel could complete his testing before all the ditches were shut down at the end of October—before the water, like sandhill cranes, went south for winter, leaving the ditches muddy and then dry until the headgates were opened again in spring.

"Kathleen!"

"Hey, Daniel, how are you? Have you met my grandson?"

Daniel leaned over and shook the little hand.

Daniel had seen Kathleen more over the years than he had seen anyone else from the old neighborhood. Jeff had been right—she was the only sane one in that unkempt house across the street. And she was the only one of the Murdocks to survive Jeff's death intact. Her parents, Fred and Dorothy, smoked and drank themselves to their graves, albeit a decade apart. And then there was Emily, a river rat in the summer who lived with strange men among the cottonwoods, a downtown dumpster denizen in the cold months of winter. But Kathleen had become a teacher, married, had children. After she retired she moved to Corrales—into an old adobe house not unlike her grandmother's along the *acequia madre*.

Yes, Kathleen was always the normal one in that house, except for Jeff, of course. When Daniel first saw her after coming home from Vietnam, she was the only one who could talk about Jeff. She even took Daniel to visit his grave, though she never knew he visited it every year thereafter on Jeff's birthday. January 15. It was just a boy's birthday until some bald man read it aloud in front of the whole country one cold December night, 1969. Jeff's birthday—that day on the calendar that took him to his death less than a year later. How many can blame their death on the date of their birth? Too many to count.

"How are your kids?" she asked, as she brushed a leaf from her grandson's hair.

"Great. But I wish they were closer."

"I know. You might just have to move one of these days, Daniel."

They laughed at the improbability of either of them leaving, as they stared off at the field of peppers and squash, ready for harvest, the Sandias in the distance.

"Who are we kidding?" he said. "You and I were born in the right place. We could never leave all this."

Daniel and Kathleen visited for a few more minutes and then he said, "You know, I saw Emily a couple weeks ago. You know she's been living in the bosque, don't you?"

"I know, and then downtown in the winter months. I've tried, Daniel, I really have." Kathleen sighed, as she looked in the direction of the river they both loved. "She knows I have an extra room here if she ever wants it."

"Well, she was always kind of different," he said.

"No kidding! Poor thing. I don't know how she ever got through high school, because she never could concentrate."

"She says she's working on a dissertation."

"Daniel, she got kicked out of UNM in her sophomore year. Then she managed to find three losers to marry. Thank goodness she never had any kids, poor thing." Kathleen looked down and kicked a rock that landed in the ditch with a splash.

"Have you tried getting her on disability or anything?"

"She won't see a doctor. You know, Daniel, my mother told me once that Emily was an accident. They had already had two kids, a boy and a girl. And then Emily came along, and maybe she was just treated differently."

"Your parents always seemed nice, though."

"I know. I don't really blame it on them, but it didn't help that she wasn't particularly planned. Plus, I know from old stories that my mother started drinking when I was just a baby. That means she was an alcoholic when she was pregnant with Emily. I've often thought maybe she suffered from fetal alcohol syndrome, even though they didn't have a name for it back then. Anyway, I meet up with her every couple of months at the post office on Broadway, if she remembers, and give her some cash and clothes. She let me take her to a dentist once, but then she wouldn't go back for the follow-up work."

Daniel saw the helplessness in Kathleen's eyes, heard the sorrow in her voice. She was the sole survivor of a family lost to bad luck, to poor choices. He put his hand on her shoulder. Thank god for the little boy whose hand she now held; thank god for all the others who came through her, for the man who shared her bed, and for the roof and sturdy walls that kept her warm and safe. Jeff would have been glad for at least one of his sisters.

"I'm sure you've tried everything," Daniel said, as her grandson started to fidget. "I'll keep an eye on Emily whenever I'm working down there. Maybe one of these days she'll take you up on your offer."

"I don't know if she'll ever be able to live inside," Kathleen said, as she started to walk away. "She'd have to give up all her so-called friends on the streets. And all she ever talks about is trying to find some man she met through the personals. I'm sure it's all in her head."

––––––––––

Daniel woke in the middle of that night, remembering the advice he had given Jacob. "You'll get through this, and then later you'll be able to help someone else," he had said, as though he had known what he was talking about. Wise words, he supposed, but advice Daniel had never heeded. His shame was short-lived that night, though, as the haggard face of Emily Murdock suddenly appeared out of the dark. If he couldn't help his own little sister, maybe he could at least help Jeff's. By the following week, Daniel was walking through the bosque in search of Emily Murdock. He found her on the same bench along Tingley Beach, picking up kernels of corn from the ground and tossing them to the grateful ducks.

"Hey, Emily, it's Daniel Arroyo. You know, from across the street. Jeff's friend?"

"Oh sure, I remember you. Have you read my dissertation? It's almost done."

"I'd like to read it. What's it about?" he said, as he took a seat on the bench next to her.

Emily scooted a few inches away, took a deep breath, and began to speak to the ground beneath her mismatched shoes, as though presenting a well-rehearsed defense before an academic committee.

"Sealed mines. When do you seal a mine after a collapse? Miners are still in there, maybe dead, maybe alive. Copper is definitely still in there, or maybe coal. When do you seal a mine? Do you wait until there is absolutely no hope? Do you seal it when the cost of rescue or recovery becomes too high? That's it. Sealed mines."

"How did you get interested in mines?" Daniel asked, as Emily took a deep breath and readied for another rapid-fire explanation.

"Well, they were all over the neighborhood. You don't remember?

Practically every house had one. You had one. It was in the backyard. Ours was on the side by the Burns."

Daniel flashed on the day he tried to coax Emily out of the Murdocks' crawl space, when she was just a little girl.

"I spent many a day in those mines," she said, looking toward the sky.

The crawl spaces. She was talking about the crawl spaces below all the houses, and she had clearly been in them more than once. They had lids, though most were flimsy enough for a young girl to lift by herself, he supposed.

"How did you get in there?" Daniel asked, incredulously.

"Mother put me in there. And Jeff let me out when he got home from school. You let me out once. I had a flashlight and crayons and my coloring book. When I got older I could get in and out myself."

Daniel's eyes stung at the thought of Emily being kept in the crawl space, and his chest tightened. Or was this even true? Dorothy Murdock drank a lot, but she was always nice to the neighborhood kids, including her own. Daniel couldn't imagine her putting Emily in there, with all the spiders and dust and old construction debris. And Jeff certainly never mentioned it. Maybe he would ask Kathleen next time he saw her.

He took a deep breath and asked, "What was in the mines?"

"Oh, the usual stuff. Copper, chunks of rock. Food wrappers from earlier shifts."

"And you went into other mines in the neighborhood?"

"Oh sure. I used to go into the Burns' mine all the time. It was nicer than ours, and I made a little tent just inside the opening. I was going to live there and be an artist, pastels. But Mr. Burns saw me one day and made me leave. He threw away my tent and put screws on the lid so I couldn't get back in. I was in your mine, too."

Daniel hadn't been in the crawl space beneath his old house since he was six, the time his father was checking for a leak. He had tried to get Jeff Murdock to go in once, but Jeff hated the crawl spaces.

"What was in there?" he asked.

"Same thing, copper and broken rock. I don't know; I haven't been in there since my teens. I think maybe a candle."

Emily's voice trailed off as she murmured, "Some other stuff."

Her words sped up again, though, as she said, "I thought about living there, too, but it was too close to the basketball court and that would have driven me crazy."

Daniel wondered what exactly did drive her crazy. Maybe Kathleen was right, it was Dorothy Murdock's alcoholism. Maybe it was nothing at all. Maybe she was just born that way. Who knows, Carmen might have turned out the same way, and no one would have ever known since she died so young. Not likely, though. No, she would have followed Daniel around, learned how to play basketball. She would still have a pretty smile and sparkly brown eyes, and a clean forehead. Her hair would have grown long, and he would have protected her from boys who weren't good enough. Later, he would have been her firstborn's godfather. No, Carmen wouldn't have been crazy.

"So, your dissertation—did you ever figure out when to seal a mine?"

"That's the last part. It's complicated, lots of factors. Economics. The human factor. I haven't decided yet, and keep rewriting the conclusion. Sometimes I say never. Just build some fence to keep the public from falling in, and wait for the miners to dig themselves out, or to rise from the dead. Other times the research leads me to say seal it after a month. If those miners haven't come out in a month, they're never coming out, period. End of story. Have you seen the latest *Alibi*? I still haven't heard back from my date, but I haven't seen this week's edition yet."

"I saw it this morning," Daniel lied. "He hasn't written back yet."

Jeff would have punched him if he had seen the disappointment on Emily's face.

"I'm sure he will one of these days, though," he said. "How about if I give you a ride to my place and fix dinner for you; would you like that?"

She actually blushed; from beneath the weathered and brown skin,

Emily Murdock actually blushed. And then she smiled and said through missing teeth, "Can we have salmon?"

She stayed in the truck while Daniel ran into the grocery store.

"This is so good, Daniel," Emily Murdock said as she took another bite of the grilled salmon, and a sip of wine. "You know, the French eat their salad after the main course," she said, staring at the still untouched plate of arugula and mixed greens at her side. "I won't have enough room for dessert if I eat any more."

"Would you like another glass of wine?"

"Oh my, no," she said. "Mother drank too much and I don't want to end up like her."

Daniel returned Emily Murdock to the bosque before dark, after she turned down his offer to sleep on the couch.

"It's going to be getting cold soon, are you sure?"

"Oh no," she replied, "never on a first date." And then she winked.

For every Saturday afternoon of that autumn, Daniel Arroyo would pick up Emily and take her to his house for a warm meal. And every Saturday evening he would return her to the safety of her bosque, before dark settled in. But when the days grew shorter and the temperatures of autumn plunged, when the blankets and coat and socks he brought her failed to keep her from the cold, one Saturday she was gone. Daniel searched the bosque, now empty except for a couple of bearded, old men, but there was no Emily. Not even a shred of the tarp and garbage bags she called her summer home deep among the cottonwoods, now bared of their leaves.

That night Daniel walked the cold streets of downtown Albuquerque, searching the alleys, looking behind the dumpsters. He even peeked in the windows of Café Benoit, though he never really expected to see her there. He finally found Emily sitting on the curb of the drive-through at Bank of America, near the post office where she would occasionally meet Kathleen for money, for clothes, for another futile invitation to move into her sister's house.

"You okay, Emily? It's Daniel."

"Oh, Daniel, I'm afraid my dissertation remains unfinished." She shivered in the cold.

"That's okay, Emily. How about coming over for something warm?"

She said nothing, but she didn't say no.

"You can bring all your things. Stay right here while I get my truck, okay?"

"This is not where I stay," she corrected him, as she pulled her wagon in the direction of the alley. "My place is around the corner."

Emily was still there when Daniel turned into the alley. She was pulling something out of the dumpster, but let it drop when the headlights hit her. Daniel opened the passenger door for her, and she winked at him as he pulled the seatbelt around her and buckled it.

"Don't forget my things," she said.

"I'm getting them right now."

Daniel loaded Emily Murdock's worldly possessions into the back of his pickup—an old wooden wagon he swore he remembered from when they were kids, a frying pan, mug, and three spoons, a pillow that had a purple cover fastened to it with rusted safety pins, some clothes, a notebook stuffed with loose papers, two ballpoint pens clipped over the final pages. He tossed the tarp over it all.

"Be careful, that's my dissertation in there. I'm almost done."

"It'll be okay. We don't have that far to go."

She seemed nervous as she looked through the back window of the cab, then into the side mirror.

"Don't worry, Emily. I'll keep it all safe."

After Daniel unloaded Emily's things and neatly placed them in one corner of the living room where she could still see them, he poured her a cup of warm tea and then heated a can of soup. He watched as she cupped her weathered hands around the steaming cup, then drank from the bowl of soup. The lines around her mouth ran deep, the bags below her blue eyes were dark. The skin on her neck hung like crepe, and her back was bowed. Is this how Jeff would have looked as an old man? Not likely. He would have had her silver hair and the same blue eyes, but his cheeks would show the color of a man who ate three meals a day, who drank water from the tap. His posture would be straight from sleeping in a warm bed next to a loving wife, his wrinkles from smiling at the children who had filled his house.

"I run into Kathleen once in a while, you know," Daniel said. "She sure would like to have you move in with her, especially now that her kids have grown."

"What happened to her husband?"

"He's still there."

"She owes me money, you know. I have to meet her every month at the post office so she can make a payment."

It seemed there was not a single aspect of Emily Murdock's life she hadn't turned around, made to appear better. A summer home, fine dinners with friends along a quiet river. A mystery date, a dissertation nearly done. A sister who owed her money. Christ, she'd been rewriting her story since she was a kid hiding in crawl spaces beneath the old houses, imagining her life as an artist below ground. What would she see in a mirror, though? How to explain weathered skin, missing teeth? Would she just look with disdain past her reflection to some strange woman who never fixed her hair, who never washed her face? Perhaps she would just stare into her own blue eyes, and hold her gaze on that one part of her that remained from childhood.

And what about Jeff? What would he have done for his sister? Hard to say. He was just an adventurous boy who didn't get to turn into a man. Hard to say.

"Well, maybe she could pay you back with free room and board," Daniel said.

Emily said nothing, but she didn't say no.

"Well, please at least stay here tonight. You can take a bath and I'll fix up the couch with some sheets and a pillow, a warm blanket. How's that sound? I promise I'll take you back tomorrow, if you still want."

Emily rolled her eyes, sighed long and loud, and then suddenly said okay. As she soaked in the warm bath he poured for her, Daniel Arroyo called Kathleen.

"You're kidding," Kathleen said on the other end of the phone. "How did you manage that?"

"Maybe she finally just got too cold. She's not young any more, you know."

An hour later, as Emily lay sleeping on her old neighbor's couch, Daniel let in Kathleen. She had brought a bag of clothes, slippers and a nightgown and robe, sneakers that she hoped would fit. Together, they watched Emily Murdock in the kind of sleep that makes the eyelids twitch, the drool fall to the pillow. The kind of sleep that lets you snore without waking even yourself.

"Did your mom ever put her in the crawl space?" Daniel asked, as he set down a Coke on the kitchen table.

"God, no," Kathleen replied. "Mom spent most of her sober hours trying to get her out of either the crawl space or the hall bathroom, and then dusting her off or wiping away all the lipstick she had smeared on the mirror."

"Well, she claims your mom put her in there, though she didn't seem particularly upset by it."

"No, that didn't happen. She was always trying to hide from everyone. Mom even had to ask Walt Burns next door to fasten down their lid so she couldn't get in. Emily had some fantasy of living in their crawl space. She'd even put some of her things down there."

That was the best news Daniel had heard all day. Dorothy Murdock was a drunk, but everyone had known that. At least she wasn't cruel. In fact, everyone in the neighborhood had liked her, except for maybe his own mother. Daniel couldn't remember her ever talking to Dorothy Murdock after Carmen died. All she did was make occasional, derisive comments about Dorothy's drinking, or not watching her kids closely enough.

"Just keep the nightgown and robe here, in case she comes back," Kathleen whispered as she and Daniel walked quietly through the living room. Emily had rolled from her side to her back. "And here's some cash for her."

"I'll keep trying to talk her into moving in with you," Daniel said in a hushed tone, as Kathleen headed to her car.

The next day Daniel gave Emily her new things, except for the nightgown and robe, which he hung in the back of his closet, and then returned her to the spot behind the dumpster in her favorite alley. He found her every night for the next six weeks, and every night he would haul her things to his apartment, fix her dinner. For six weeks, Emily Murdock bathed every night. And every night for six weeks she slept on her back in a cotton nightgown under a pink blanket on Daniel Arroyo's couch. Daniel drove her back to her alley every morning, though each time Emily would stay a little longer at his house, drink another cup of coffee, until one December morning, just before Christmas, she said, "Maybe you could drive me to Kathleen's."

Surrender the Sea

A WOODEN FENCE STILL surrounded the property, likely in its third
or fourth incarnation after all the years. As Daniel Arroyo turned
the corner onto the street he first saw the cottonwood, tall and twisted,
now missing the lateral trunk that used to hang perilously over the
fence and practically onto Helen Sedillo's front porch. That trunk had
been the only path from his yard into the old tree, and he wondered
how long its upper branches had missed the weight of some boy playing
hide-and-seek, or maybe just daydreaming—trying to get a little peace.

The Murdock house looked the same, at least from the outside,
though the lawn appeared freshly mowed. Daniel imagined a happier
family within its walls, this time with no lost little girl who ended up
a woman gone old before her time, a girl who hid in the neighborhood
crawl spaces only to become a woman living among the salt cedar along
the river, just two miles away. This time with a sober mother. He imagined a family intact, with no lost boy. Jeff's willow tree was still in the
front yard, older, taller. It had easily outlived the boy who spent summer days cradled in its highest limbs.

Daniel almost smiled at the Burns' once pristine place, set between
the Connors' and the Murdocks', always the nicest house on the block,

its yard now filled with weeds, the front screen door hanging loose from its hinges, duct tape holding a piece of cardboard over a broken window pane. He could almost hear Marge Burns barking orders at some gardener or handyman—clean this place up. Her voice would ricochet off the bare walls and echo through the cavernous corridors of the nursing home her sons had moved her to. Later, he imagined, Marge's familiar shrill would rise from her untended grave.

Two teenaged girls stood across the street in the Murdocks' driveway, Jeff's driveway. They were talking through the window not of a '54 Ford Customline but of some other teen's pride and joy, a royal blue muscle car with black stripes and multicolored decals, the sound of its running engine rising above their laughter. As Daniel parked along the curb, the girls' mother called out the door for them to come inside—some mother not Dorothy, drowned in alcohol just three years before. Daniel sat in his pickup truck and watched the teenaged boy leave, stereo blasting. His own engine still idled in front of the old North Valley house, as though his truck might suddenly decide this was a bad idea, and drive him away.

Ever since Helen had called him and said that the people who lived in his old house had found something he had to see, Daniel knew he would have to return to the neighborhood.

"Can't we just meet somewhere else, like the Flying Star?" Daniel had implored Helen Sedillo. "Can't you just bring whatever it is you want me to see?"

"No," she had said. "You have to come over here."

Daniel shut down his engine and sat in the truck for nearly five minutes, though it could have been fifty years. He was just a few feet from where his mother had wailed one awful afternoon and rolled in agony beneath the cottonwood; just a few feet from the gate she had crashed through. He could still see her falling onto the sidewalk and then into the gutter that ran with water from a late August thunderstorm, her pink housedress turning a muddy brown. Here he was, just a few feet from the back of a driveway out of which had lurched an old, blue Chevy station wagon, Miguel Arroyo's panicked face at the driver's window, Helen Sedillo's head bent too late over a baby named Carmen.

Now the gutter was dry and clean, and day lilies lined the fence and bloomed above a host of flowering perennials that bordered the sidewalk in every color imaginable. The driveway held not a blue Chevy station wagon but a green Honda Civic, recently waxed. Two ristras hung in a welcoming pose on either side of the gate, and Daniel thought he heard music coming through an open front door. His door, through which he would soon enter as a stranger.

The years had scattered the cast of his childhood like dust along a ditch in a spring wind, rendered some of them ghosts. Daniel and a few others had settled nearby, but most had landed in other towns, other states, where different children climbed younger trees. The wind had blown two teenaged boys like tumbleweeds to the opposite side of the planet, mercifully blew one home. It had sent many in the old neighborhood to their graves, some too soon. But it had also scattered seeds, made room for new lives in old houses.

All that remained was Helen Sedillo, widowed and grown old now, her boys scattered across the West, her girl somewhere in Boston. Daniel took a deep breath and then walked quickly to her door, rang the bell before he had a chance to turn around. After what he imagined was a slow walk across her living room, Helen opened the door not tentatively, but with the same enthusiasm she always had.

"Daniel Arroyo, I thought you'd never get out of that truck!" she laughed. "Get in here and give me a hug! I've been so looking forward to this."

She must be in her eighties now, Daniel thought. Her hair was solid silver, though still long and pulled up in a bun on the back of her head. She seemed shorter, maybe a little thinner. But her voice remained strong, her laugh contagious. Helen Sedillo had always been the anchor of the neighborhood, the link between the adults and the kids.

Children would let family secrets slip across the Sedillos' kitchen table while drinking Cokes after a summer afternoon of riding bikes, or playing basketball. And parents would call asking if she had seen their children, then lower their voices and talk of trouble at home. Please don't tell anyone, they would say. Helen never did. She was the keeper of their stories, and she had outlasted them all.

"You look great," Daniel said, as he took a seat in the same recliner chair in front of the television where Mr. Sedillo would fall asleep every night. Helen returned from the kitchen with two cookies on a paper napkin, and a glass of iced tea.

"Marty and David catch me up on everyone now and then," she said, smiling. "But I don't even remember the last time I saw you in person."

"I think it was right after I got out of the army. I had come over to see the Murdocks, and you and Mr. Sedillo were out in the driveway."

"Oh, I can still picture that Jeff. What a stinker he could be—jumping out of that old willow like he could fly. He gave Dorothy and Fred fits. Do you remember when he crashed the car into that arroyo in the foothills?"

Daniel just smiled and nodded, looked at the floor.

"Well, he was always polite," she said quietly. "What a shame...," her voice trailed off.

Yes, it was all shameful, Daniel thought. A generation of boys sent halfway around the world, for no good reason, and all because they couldn't afford to hide in college somewhere. And when the country ran short on those boys, it held a lottery like a TV game show where the winning contestant got a free vacation to some exotic destination. Yes, it was absolutely a shame.

"I was so sorry to hear about your mother. I was just too sick to go to the mass that day."

"Thanks. She'd been ready to go for a long time."

"So tell me about yourself, Daniel. How are the kids? Marty says your son is in the service."

He wondered if Helen had already heard about his divorce from Laura.

"Jacob is still in the army," he said. "He's a corporal at Fort Bragg, doing security training. You knew he had gone to Iraq, didn't you?"

Helen nodded.

"He did almost three tours there. And Molly is married and in southern California. I'm actually a grandfather now, a girl. Can you believe it?"

"Well, Marty and David are both grandfathers now too," she said.

She went on, telling Daniel about her children. Her boys had become plumbers and teachers and policemen, had married and divorced and married again. Marty, who lived in a Sandia mountain town that didn't even exist when they were kids, still had season tickets for the Lobos basketball games. Her only daughter had gone off long ago with a college English professor and lived outside of Boston in a world even farther away.

"What kind of work do you do? Marty says it has something to do with the river."

He told her about going to college on the GI bill, about his work as a hydrogeological technician, of taking the measure of the Rio Grande from its headwaters to the Gulf.

"I run across Kathleen Murdock on the Corrales ditch once in a while. She has a grandson, you know," he said.

And then Daniel told Helen of Kathleen's little sister, Emily, lost to the streets, lost to the salt cedar along the river.

"I know. I'd heard that from Marty."

"Well, the good news is she started letting me bring her over for dinner. And after a while she started spending the nights at my place."

"What?" Helen said, surprised.

"Kathleen knew," he added quickly. "And then one morning she finally let me take her to Kathleen's house. She's living there now."

"Well, bless her heart," Helen said. "She was such a strange little thing. I'm glad she's safe, though, and I'm sure her folks are breathing a sigh of relief. Jeff too." She took a sip of tea. "What about all the Arroyos? Where's Michael?"

Daniel told her about his older brother, who had finally settled down in Belen and who had a construction business, five grandchildren, and the same wife. What about Anna, she wanted to know. And Lisa and Joey. She asked about all of them, save that one whom they always talked circles around, as though she was Vietnam herself, or as though she might still be next door. As though she might somehow overhear.

"I guess you know that Laura Patrick and I divorced."

She did.

Daniel never mentioned a handsome lawyer who had killed himself at the top of his stairs, just a few feet from an Italian platform bed with a headboard made of white leather. He never told her that he had carved Jeff Murdock's initials into a banyan tree the day after he received the letter saying Jeff had been killed, or that he left flowers every year on his grave.

"Do you want any more tea?" Helen offered. "Or are you ready to go next door?"

"Are you sure it's okay with her?" Daniel asked.

"I'm positive. They're very nice neighbors and take such good care of the place. And she's been so respectful about … well, you know … what she found."

But Daniel wasn't ready, and so he stalled. Who had lived there over the years, he wanted to know. Tell me a little more about the people in there now, he asked, as the butterflies in his stomach turned into a seething swarm of bees.

So Helen told Daniel of the odd artist who had lived there after his family had left and who was responsible for knocking down a wall between the two back bedrooms to make a large studio for herself. She told him of the snobbish woman from California who had planted a thorny hedge along the fence to keep out the drunks, or so she had claimed, but who never acknowledged that it was really not a matter of drunkenness but of skin tones, and of jobs that left your clothes smelling, dirt under your fingernails, and bones so tired all you wanted was a cold beer or two at the end of a hard day. And then Helen told him about the friendly couple who lived there now—the woman whose curiosity had caused her to crawl under the house after a phone repairman had made some comment about something stashed in there.

"You're coming with me, right?" Daniel finally asked.

"Absolutely," Helen said as she rose from her chair and grabbed her keys. "Don't worry so much," she said, as they walked through Daniel's old front gate. "It'll be fine. I promise."

The woman who opened the door was close to his own age, with eyes not unlike his grandmother's, and a nice smile. He relaxed for just a moment.

"You must be Daniel Arroyo," she said, before Helen even had a chance to introduce them. "Please, come in."

Daniel stood silent in the living room and looked up, while Helen went into the kitchen for a glass of water. The wood ceiling was even darker than he had remembered, but the walls were still of warm plaster, the oak floors still a beautiful gold, quartersawn. He could almost see the green velvet couch. The casement windows had been replaced, along with the screen door, and curtains exchanged for wooden blinds. The hall seemed shorter in distance, but also appeared to reach farther than he could have ever imagined. Daniel's throat went tight as he recalled the memory that lay at the end of that hall, through the last door on the right.

He accepted a glass of water from the woman.

Someone had knocked out half the wall between the kitchen and dining room, opening it up and making both rooms seem much larger. And lighter; it was so light. Then he noticed the skylight that had been punched through the dark ceiling. Gone was the old stove, a green Viking in its place, a dishwasher. The tiles had been changed, though were still talavera.

"Feel free to walk around," the woman said. "I even cleaned," she laughed.

Daniel walked slowly past the kitchen doorway on his left and the first little bedroom on the right where he and his brothers had laughed late into summer nights, past the door upon which his father had knocked the evening of December 1, 1969. "Daniel, they called your number." He had barely heard his dad over Jimi Hendrix's guitar screaming through the transistor radio.

The bathroom on the left, the one with the tub he had shared with all his brothers and sisters and grandmother, looked much smaller. Gone was the pink toilet, replaced by a low-flow with a wooden seat. The tub had been refinished in a creamy yellow, though some soap bar had gone dry and stuck to the finish, pulling away the yellow and showing an uneven blotch of the pink surface he had remembered. Someone had tiled the tub and sink area.

Daniel felt nearly sick as he approached the end of the hall. He looked to his left, into his parents' bedroom where Dolores Arroyo had napped that day. "Don't bother Carmen," she had said, ". . . be quiet so I can get some sleep." The words screamed at him from across the years.

He made himself look to the right, noticing first that there was only one doorway where two had been. The hall was shorter; he hadn't just imagined it. He walked into the now long room, which used to be two bedrooms—until an artist had removed the wall between them and plastered off the last doorway. The first room would have been his sisters', and he could almost hear the two of them laughing as they knocked on the wall of the boys' room late one night, and made ghostly sounds through the heater duct on the floor—until they all realized the same noises traveled through the ductwork into all the rooms, including Miguel and Dolores Arroyo's room. "Go to bed!" they all heard their father's booming voice echo through the floor ducts.

And then he was finally there, standing in what was the last bedroom on the right—his grandmother's room and whatever baby who was still too young to be with older sisters, or older brothers. Carmen's room. The sun was shining through the west window just like it had that August afternoon. He looked out the window and saw a backyard filled with flowers and brick planters. Gone was the concrete basketball court, the backboard. But a wild rose still grew beneath the window, the same wild rose from all those years ago, he imagined. Inside, a computer desk and bookshelves in place of a crib, a file cabinet where an oak nightstand with a rosary upon it once stood.

Daniel tried to take a sip of his water, but it fell over his bottom lip and down his shirt. Helen and the other woman pretended not to see, but he had to leave the room.

The younger woman offered him some tea, but he just took more water and asked if he could walk around the yard. They went out the front door, and Daniel slowly approached the old cottonwood. He walked a half circle around its huge trunk, then stopped where he saw her initials carved just under the lowest limb. The tree had bled into the letters over the years, making them hard to distinguish from the bark. Daniel brushed away an old spiderweb on the C and thought briefly of a J etched into some banyan tree on the other side of the world.

"Can we go into the backyard now?"

Daniel's pace quickened as they walked around the side of the house. The four elms were still there, taller now but casting familiar shadows across what used to be the basketball court. Just as he pictured Jeff Murdock missing that last shot, Daniel heard a familiar sound and turned to see the woman lifting the cover to the crawl space.

"Whenever you're ready," she said, as she handed him a flashlight. "Go about eight feet, and then over to the west wall, just below where the window and the rose would be."

Daniel stared at the opening and said nothing.

"I put everything back exactly where I found it," she said quietly. "I'm going into the house now. Take your time."

Daniel and Helen stood in silence.

"Go ahead, Daniel."

After another pause, Daniel rolled up his sleeves and stepped down toward the opening of the crawl space, got on his knees, and headed in.

He swept the beam of the flashlight back and forth across the bottom of the west wall, until a reflection caught his eye. It was the clasp of a metal box, and it pulled at him like a magnet. His hands and knees tossed up dust as he crawled without hesitation toward the spot along the wall.

The metal box was tarnished and dull, and not familiar to him. Who knows, it could have been in the far reaches of the garage with Miguel's tools, hidden behind the more interesting jars of screws and nails, washers, and other miscellaneous hardware Daniel used to get into. A glass candle stood in front of the box, the kind they sold at the old neighborhood grocery store in the aisle next to the beer. Its paint was faded but still showed a vague outline of the Virgin of Guadalupe, now covered in dust and cobwebs.

Daniel fidgeted with the clasp, and slowly lifted the lid of the box. His neck stiffened and he held his head back as though some ghost might jump out. But there was no ghost, just a swatch of a cotton blanket, its pink flowers nearly faded away. Carmen's blanket. Daniel wiped off his hands, then picked up the cotton swatch. He felt its softness between his fingers, held it to his nose as though the scent of his baby sister had somehow lingered after all these years. A white rosary was wrapped inside the cloth, along with a black-and-white photograph, its edges worn as if from too much handling. It showed a beaming Miguel Arroyo holding his baby girl under the cottonwood tree. And then a flood of memories—the day the family left for the vacation in San Diego, the strange sound from the backyard, the glimpse through the gap in the fence, his father walking away from the crawl space and wiping his eyes.

As Daniel returned the cloth to the box, his ring finger brushed across another object, causing it to move. The sound of metal on metal. The flashlight beam revealed a small steel rectangle showing Murdock on the first line, Jeffrey A. just below. Jeff's dog tag, the one that came home with him. Emily must have put it there. A spot of Mekong mud, now gone to dust, still covered part of the number on the third line.

Daniel emerged ten minutes later, wearing a tarnished dog tag and cradling a closed metal box and glass candle close to his chest. Muddy streaks lined his face, where old tears had met even older dust. Helen Sedillo was waiting for him.

"I went into her room, and she was fine. She even smiled at me. I held her for a minute, then put her down again the way Mom had showed me, and went outside to play more basketball. It started getting cloudy, and there was a little thunder in the distance. So I went back in to check on her."

Helen's eyes filled with tears, as Daniel looked to the ground.

"The blanket had slipped, and her diaper might have been wet, but she was still sleeping. So I patted her back for a minute, but she still didn't wake up. And then I picked her up."

He patted her back. Good God, thought Helen, she had already turned herself over in the crib.

"Since it was close to the time my mom or grandmother would wake her, I thought it would be okay to take her outside. She didn't wake up, though, even when I held her," he choked, his voice cracking and heavy with sorrow.

"I thought I would just take her around to see the ditch. I even held some asparagus to her nose, and she still didn't wake up, so then I pretended to baptize her. She had slept through her own baptism at Sacred Heart, you know, even when Father Baca sprinkled the water on her."

The mud on the forehead, thought Helen.

"I swear, I never touched her mouth or got her face or nose anywhere near the water. I wiped her forehead with my shirt and then carried her back to the house, but I didn't wake Mom. I put her back in the crib and pulled the blanket up, but I had put her on her side. She must have rolled over onto her stomach and suffocated. I didn't know anything was wrong, and Mom was still asleep."

A single tear spilled from the corner of Helen's left eye and rolled down her cheek.

"Daniel, she had already been on her stomach when you picked her up. Didn't you just hear yourself? You patted her back before you ever picked her up. It wasn't your fault, Daniel."

"Yes it was. I shouldn't have taken her to the ditch, and I was the one who put her on her side."

"She was already gone when you took her to the ditch, Daniel. When your father handed her to me, she was already blue. She had been gone for quite a while. Besides, don't you remember the phone ringing?" Helen asked.

"No, what phone? I had gone back outside to shoot baskets."

"The phone woke your mother, and she thought Carmen was fine."

"What do you mean? I didn't hear anything until Mom started yelling her name. That's when me and Michael ran in, right before Dad got home."

"Daniel," Helen said softly, "Dorothy Murdock called that afternoon and woke your mother. She had tripped in the kitchen and asked your mom to bring over some hydrogen peroxide for the cut on her head. Your mom glanced into Carmen's room and thought she was fine, because she was on her side."

"I don't get what you're saying."

"Daniel, your mother ran over to the Murdocks' house. But just as she got there, Dorothy threw up. She had been drinking, and your mother helped her clean up before Fred got home from work. And then she had to talk little Emily out of the bathroom. She had locked herself in. Anyway, by the time she got back to the house, your mother couldn't wake her."

"How do you know all this?" Daniel asked incredulously.

"Your mother told me, a week after Jeff was killed. She blurted out something like you reap what you sow, though I don't think she really meant to be so harsh. But Dorothy had already told me years earlier how guilty she had felt about having called your mother away that afternoon. I think your mother felt guilty, too."

The day went silent.

How could so many be so guilty, Daniel thought. They couldn't. A tired mother puts a plastic sheet in her baby's crib to save the mattress below. A young boy picks up his tiny sister as thunder approaches from the distance, then he lays her back down. The baby somehow manages to turn onto her stomach. Too much time passes. The boy then carries her to the ditch, tries to wake her with the sweet smell of wild asparagus. "In the name of the Father, and of the Son, and of the Holy Spirit," he says, as he anoints her little forehead in water brown with mud. He then carries the baby back to her room, and lays her down with as much care as he knows how. Something in the house across the street causes a nice neighbor to drink too much, a two-year-old to lock herself in the bathroom. When do you seal a mine? Fathers are coming home from long days at work, mothers and grandmothers are starting dinner. Children splash each other in gutters wet from a summer rain. Some play basketball, some climb trees.

They are all guilty, they are all blameless.

Daniel Arroyo drove around the street corner slowly, the metal box and glass candle resting safe on the passenger seat next to him, the dog tag hanging on the rearview mirror as a reminder to take it to Kathleen. He had returned Emily to her, now he could at least give back what remained of Jeff.

The truck practically parked itself alongside the fence behind the old house, and Daniel got out. The wild asparagus above the ditch smelled as sweet as ever. How many times had he sat hidden among its green ferns; how many times had he dangled his bare feet in the water below? Did the ditch bank still know him; did it recognize the pace of his steps? Maybe. Had the tears he wept the day Carmen died fallen into the water and made their way to the Rio Grande? Had he caused the river to register a higher level, a stronger flow? Daniel peeked through the gap in the fence. The backyard was empty; the woman had replaced the cover to the crawl space, sealed the mine. He looked skyward to an abundant, blue canvas waiting to be filled with sandhill cranes flying south to their winter home. He would save that place in the sky, his feet on solid ground now, until the song of the cranes rose in the distance of some October morning.

PART TWO

The River Flyway

Quartersawn Century

The Dining Table

My chairs went missing just west of Kansas City on a blazing August afternoon. Stacked unceremoniously next to a flowered sofa at the barn's edge, their backs to the auctioneer, they were easily passed over by the dealer from Colorado. For seventy-five years I have longed for their dark arrow spindles, rising above sunken seat centers to meet delicate crests carved deep with laurel wreaths, edged with scrolls known only to the strong hands of some turn-of-the-century furniture maker, long dust beneath a red oak near Syracuse, squirrels picking at the acorns scattered across his untended grave.

Now Daniel Arroyo sits in one of four mismatched chairs, his sharp features gone obtuse in the elongating shadows cast about this room, the silver of his hair lost to the backlight from the western window. His wife, Laura, is seated across from him and he cannot help but notice her blue eyes gaze at something just beyond his shoulder when he speaks, perhaps the leaves of the Japanese maple going curled and brown beneath the hot New Mexico sun, a car passing slowly by. He does not know when she lost interest, only that she did sometime between 1972, when his welcome knee brushed against hers as they ate the pork tenderloin his mother had cooked in honor of their engagement, and two years ago when he stretched his legs one night at dinner and her foot recoiled at his accidental touch.

Their daughter, seated at Laura's right, twists her hair through her fingers and rearranges the asparagus into an accusatory arrow on her plate. She jumps from her chair with gratitude at the ringing of her cell phone. No one speaks of or dares even look in the direction of the fourth chair, empty—the chair that once held the boy with the two long legs, legs that kicked at his younger sister, that rose strong from feet tapping private melodies, that made a lap for his napkin to hold the peas he never learned to like—legs that now wearily shuffle along some ruined road leading from Baghdad. His chair now sits at an angle and holds unread magazines, *Seventeen* and *People*, the occasional *Time*, as though the reminder of a missed boy could be papered over, hidden beneath glossy covers painted with garishly perfect faces, or buried under the austere stares of the mighty.

I hold all the private prayers for that boy, and when he returns home some warm April day, his army stripes traded for a blue swaddling blanket draped over his shoulder, I shall hold his boy. I am fine timber oak, durable and strong. My legs reach far from center post; they rest firm on great lion's paw feet, fear no collapse. I bear the weight of a century—the old wars with the Great Depression in between, Daniel Arroyo's war, the prosperous times, the new battles. History reflects off my surface like candlelight on fine china; it goes hidden between my leaves in the small crumbs of a person's day.

I have set a place for all who have come before—the wealthy man from Chicago who first bought me off the pages of the 1900 Sears catalogue as a gift for his daughter and her new husband, a Kansas farmer she had met on the train, their five children. For thirty years I stood reluctant witness before a drafty window that looked upon the vast, empty prairie that alternately swallowed its people or spit them out, one by one, until the farmhouse went forever silent on a bitter December night. After a short time with a coal speculator gone broke, Daniel

Arroyo's grandparents came upon me in a warehouse in southern Colorado. It was late 1931; Daniel's mother still fed at her own mother's breast, still had two older brothers. Many years later I made my way to New Mexico with Daniel's young parents, strapped to the bed of an old Ford pickup, a blanketed mirror wedged safely between me and a chest of drawers. The truck rattled and bumped all the way south, until it finally came to rest in Albuquerque. My third leg still bears the scratches from a nightstand some neighbor failed to securely tie down.

I have known Daniel Arroyo all his life.

When he was a boy, he took his mother's red lipstick and traced a heart on my underside, which he quickly wiped away with a dishcloth. The night before his first date, he scratched so hard at his knee that it bled into his napkin. His fingers would stroke the keys of an imaginary piano when his mother spoke; his right foot would twitch as his father said grace. But when he came home from Vietnam, his hands lay folded and still in his lap, his feet pressed close together and tight to the floor. He married Laura Patrick the next year.

Laura's hair, once thick and red, now hangs limp in dull wisps upon her tired shoulders as she leans over the kitchen sink. Daniel failed to notice they had finished eating a half hour ago, never saw her clear the table. It was once his job to scrape the plates, but he has long forgotten, so seldom do they share a meal. Daniel usually eats late and alone now. He grinds his elbows into me and puts his head in his hands when no one else is around. I have absorbed a thousand tears—his on the day of his baby sister's funeral mass, his grandmother's when her beloved husband died, some Kansas farmer's wife after she buried her second son in a barren, unforgiving prairie. A burn spot near Daniel's left hand marks the ash that fell from his father's last cigarette, the day he made the deal with God he would quit smoking in exchange for Daniel's safe delivery from Vietnam. Maybe he should have made his own deal with God, Daniel thinks.

I am quartersawn, cut on the diagonal. My years run across the grain, from heart to bark, laid open for any to see. Untold words have made their way over my surface, some smooth as glass, others crashing upon me and falling dead on the floor. My underbelly bears witness to the small gestures, the hidden meanings. When children tell lies, they hide their hands in their laps and tear at their fingernails. When men and women speak a hard truth, they do the same. I have heard them all. But mostly I have gathered the transitory talk of ordinary people living ordinary lives. How was your day? Please pass the bread.

The Gentleman's Chest

I ARRIVED IN the middle of a blizzard, the first of my kind born of the Heinrich furniture-making colony in Syracuse. Dried in a kiln and swaddled in steam, I took form beneath the able hands of Franz Heinrich. He sanded open my pores and fed me orange shellac with yellow ochre pigment, then added the nut-brown stain that still causes appreciative hands to stroke my scalloped shelfback and dovetailed drawers. And then he bestowed upon me my first secret, four tiny initials carved inside a heart behind the apron, where no one could see.

Now I keep safe Daniel's secrets. For thirty-five years he faithfully placed Laura's letters in the bottom of the third drawer, behind the T-shirts and on top of a mass card for his dead baby sister, to join the boutonnière he wore at their wedding and a rose she handed him on their first anniversary, its petals gone cracked and dry. Over time, the flowers fell into the gap between the drawers and the letters went covered by unmatched socks and Father's Day ties, which he soon buried beneath an old pair of jeans.

But late one night he added a business card with a photograph of a handsome lawyer, words written on the back, "Call anytime," and a telephone number. Daniel had not meant for anything to happen; all he wanted was a cold beer in a dark, cool place before returning home. He had not realized his was a heart in search of comfort, until a second beer mysteriously appeared in front of him, followed by a voice to his left, deep and kind.

"You look like you could use a friend."

The man's house lit a flame in the pit of Daniel Arroyo's stomach that spread across his senses like a cleansing spring wildfire, from the moment the key turned in the door to an hour later when he sat on the edge of an Italian platform bed with a white leather headboard, and slipped on the shoes he had placed beneath the attached nightstand. Fine, abstract lithographs reached out from living room walls, an acrylic bistro table held glasses of smooth French wine that reflected in the candlelight. They sat upon matching chairs with chrome legs, then walked past a frameless octagonal mirror, and climbed wooden stairs one anticipatory step at a time to a bedroom draped in bold tapestries and filled with the pulse of unfamiliar music that poured from speakers perched high upon stackable dressers. There were no ghosts in this place—no dead babies, no best friend from across the street, no boys slaughtered in jungles on the other side of the planet.

Daniel returned home late that night, said something about an unexpected dinner meeting, and tucked the business card into the drawer.

I am blood of a southern acorn, a great sawlog shipped north, destined to be a keeper of secrets. If Daniel Arroyo ever pulled out my second drawer, he would find a torn piece of a once cigar-shaped cellophane wrapper his twelve-year-old mother hid there in the summer of 1943, just before her brother went off to war. The night before he shipped out, he had unsealed the wrapper in the dim light of an oil lamp to reveal not a cigar but an official dress tie of the United States Marine Corps, narrow and red. He handed the cellophane to Daniel's mother as he finished dressing for his date and said, "Throw this away for me, will you?" In the immeasurable space of that moment, Daniel's mother knew she would never see her brother again. So she placed the wrapper in a back corner of the second drawer, the gold emblem of the marines face down. Years after her death, Laura cleaned out the drawer and, not knowing what it meant, the marine emblem erased by the years, threw away the wrapper, leaving only a small scrap stuck to the back.

And if Daniel ever placed his nose deep into the top drawer, he would smell the tobacco some Kansas farmer put in his pipe each night after slamming his wife up against the bedroom wall. But deeper still remains a single bead of rubber cement, now gone hard and dull, that once held fast a photograph of the farmer's second son, taken the summer before he took his last breath in some trench south of Strasbourg. The farmer pulled it out Christmas Eve of 1930, a few months after his wife died. He sat alone at the oak dining table with the faded image of his second son and a flask of corn whiskey late into the night, his thumb alternately rubbing the dust from the picture and then from the table, and then he took the shotgun from next to the door and put it unceremoniously beneath his whiskered chin and fired. His middle daughter cleaned off the floor and table and wall the following spring, sold the farm, except for the acre surrounding the family graves, and sent all the furniture to auction in Kansas City.

I am quartersawn, silent as timber. I reveal nothing—just a web of medullary rays, the maze of me, pith to rind. My cabriole legs steadily bear the weight of a hundred secrets. And though my keys have long vanished, if handled delicately my brass pulls stop short of striking the escutcheons, stop short of letting slip confidences. My four drawers move silently between my paneled sides; they make not a sound, even when rummaged through in the middle of sleepless nights.

The Mirror

I WAS MEANT to hold a painting. The furniture maker imagined some watercolor of a pond with wood ducks and Canada geese, a yellow warbler atop a stripped hawthorn at the water's edge. The sky would be the pink and gray of an October sunrise, the background a stand of red oak into which a path barely visible through the fallen leaves meandered, soon to be lost to the first snow. The only hint of what I was to become—a small flash of light reflecting off the pond's surface, its source known only to the artist.

Now Daniel Arroyo looks at me and sees just the left side of his face. He focuses on the cheekbone and wonders why it is slightly higher than the other side, causing a perpetual puffiness under his eye. It displeases him five times a day. He cannot see the wholeness of his face for the asymmetry of his cheekbone. He wonders if the handsome lawyer noticed. I am Daniel's memory of himself, and a reminder of who he has become. When he was young, he would part his hair to the left, splash cool water upon his face, carefully shave. Now he looks at me with disdain. Who the hell do you think you are, he wonders, his eyes puffy, his beard rough and hair disheveled from another sleepless night.

I have fielded great disappointments, thrown back cruel insults. "You selfish son of a bitch," he whispered, upon his return from the lawyer's house. "You weak bastard," he said through clenched teeth.

I was meant to hold a painting. Instead, I became a discordant collage of faces, with no face of my own. On my right edge I carry the steely, shameless glance of a farmer as he steps into a Kansas blizzard to water the cows. Some auctioneer stood before me twenty years later and slicked back his hair, just before the bidding began. I bear witness to small vanities, and to introspections so close that the fog of breath is laid upon me. I see unspeakable acts from across a darkened room; I behold boundless kindnesses awash in candlelight. Daniel's young grandfather used to suddenly appear behind his grandmother and put his arms around her as she leaned over the washbasin. She would raise her head and smile, then follow his reflection until he walked from view. She would have smiled at him for fifty years, if given the chance. And once, when no one was around, Daniel's father looked squarely into his own eyes and said, "Please, God, let him come home alive." He didn't know to ask Vietnam to stay behind.

Yes, I was meant to hold a painting. But a Kansas farmwife glued a portrait of her parents to my gilt liner that was too narrow and kept going crooked. One hot summer night the farmer smashed the glass and ripped the portrait, leaving his wife's parents, and then his wife, in tattered heaps on the floor. But I am quartersawn oak, a stable cut, tough-grained. The farmer took me to town the next day and bought a plate of beveled glass cut perfect to fit. He gave it to his wife, along with four yards of red gingham for a new summer dress.

I was meant to hold a painting. Instead, I went invisible. Those who look at me cannot see past themselves, cannot see me. A desperate man steals one last glance before he walks away, pretends I somehow absorb only him, and not the shadow of guilt he casts onto the wall behind him. Later, as I hang on some other wall, a weathered woman lingers, studies the lines on her face and the gaps in her teeth, and wonders where she went. But reflection is a heavy burden. It causes the hook to bend, rips me from the plaster, renders me a thousand pieces on the floor. So I become a daughter of deflection, waiting for some unknown man to look just past himself, to notice the wave of my grain, the carved leaves falling away from my dovetailed corners—some man who will carefully replace the glass with a bold image, who will move me to a new room, place me high upon a freshly painted wall, light a fire that flickers across my face deep into the night.

The Nightstand

I AM THE third one in the bed. I lie not between them but just to his left. When at long last they decided to have children, he would wake as the first light shone through the gap in the curtain, rub his eyes, roll onto his side and reach for her. Now I watch from my vantage and see his face contorted in a restless sleep. The glow from the digital clock taunts him, as he wakes every hour. He flips onto his back, stares toward the ceiling, and tries to convince himself to leave before turning his wife into a demon, their home into a house of horrors.

I see best in the dark, or in the opacity just before dawn. I was the only one in the room, darkened by an approaching thunderstorm, when a baby girl named Carmen took her last breath. She never knew her eight-year-old brother walked in shortly after that. She never knew he picked her up and left the room. But I did; I saw it all. And when Daniel was fourteen, his grandmother would reach for a rosary hidden behind the base of the lamp as soon as Miguel Arroyo would begin to snore in the room across the hall. As each bead passed between her fingers, she would add a special prayer for her grandson. The rosary was left behind at some funeral home a couple of years later and replaced by a crucifix just before Daniel went to Vietnam, its cross of wrought iron, its Christ of rose quartz. I have held relics from across the ages. Daniel's other grandmother placed a blue, handblown bud vase upon me in the spring of 1949. Every day for three months, as I kept watch over her beloved, his lungs gone black and marbled, she put a fresh flower in the vase—daffodils from just off the porch, then red tulips, columbine, and finally, the first of the wild roses. In the middle of a June night, as she slept in the rocker beneath the window, the curtain lace moving like a specter in the quiet breeze, he fell into a death rattle that went unheard by all but me. I watched over him until the sun came through the window, and she woke to her first day alone. I am both steadfast witness, and reluctant bystander. A foul-smelling farmer from Kansas bedded nameless women at my side on Sunday mornings, while his wife and four surviving children sat with heads bowed in prayer, or maybe shame, in the last pew at First Baptist, just outside Topeka.

When Daniel dreams now, his brow furrows deep, his face twitches. He's in some boat adrift on some ocean where the sun never sets. He's lost in his own house, going in circles, trying to remember secret passages to untroubled rooms he and Laura once occupied. He's trying to run, but his feet won't move under the weight of his heart. But just last night he dreamed he was swimming upstream, a northern pike on his way to spawn and then drown in a baptism of death. He struggled against the current, and when the river went dry he flopped through her mud and sand, until he was engulfed by the rapids of the Taos Box, where he suddenly turned into a man. He bounced off boulders and was nearly swallowed by eddies of angry, roiling water, but kept coming up for air until he reached the calm of the San Luis valley. Still, he could not rest, could not let himself be carried downstream just to be dumped unceremoniously into some sea. He swam upward through dark forests of mighty spruce and fir that lined steep canyon walls, until he reached the headwaters of the Rio Grande—a gurgling stream that spilled out of the San Juans, a stream so clear he could see beyond every reflection he had ever cast. And there, mirrored in the water just behind his right shoulder, appeared not who he had waited for, but who had waited for him.

I hid like a badger in the brush; I saw it all.

I am a simple tabouret, quartersawn. Though my scrap lays waste on the sawmill floor, I make no apology for taking more of the tree; I carry no shame for being offspring of a smaller yield. For I bear the burden of having no fear of the dark, of being a gatherer of dreams, a night raven whose cries go unheard. My surface is scarred with the stuff of nights spanning a century—the shadow of a water ring from an old blue vase, a scratch where delicate hands fumbled in the dark for some iron cross, a drop of wax from a candle long melted.

Daniel Arroyo wakes in the dark now. He slips out of bed as Laura pretends to sleep, then feels his way down the hall, past his daughter's closed door, to the phone in the study that once held his boy. "Call anytime," the lawyer had written on the back of his card. Comfort draws Daniel's fingers to the phone, answers in a deep baritone on the other end. Quiet words are exchanged, a receiver put down silently in its cradle. Daniel stands at the bedroom door, listens for the steady rhythm of Laura's breath. The clock reads 3:21. He shaves in the dark, with just the light from the streetlamp reflecting off the mirror. The bottom drawer of the gentleman's chest is silent as Daniel pulls out a fresh shirt. He scribbles a note, which he leaves on the kitchen counter. The dining table hands him his keys for the last time, and he goes quietly into the night.

The Keeper of Mortandad Canyon

H<small>E SAYS WE</small> are all soldiers now, that he cannot leave. Two years ago he said it was because of the fire, three years before that he came home and exclaimed, "TA-50 is mine!" I should know better than to bring up leaving Los Alamos. He looks just beyond me at these times, somewhere left of my face to a middle distance all his own, somewhere between me and the kitchen wall we painted last summer. His blue eyes have gone nearly gray, they peer from behind thicker lenses now and, as he mutters something about living downstream of Oak Ridge, or next to Rocky Flats, I find myself looking at his forearms and thinking he has become more hairy. I sometimes wonder if he has more hair, if the texture has changed, grown more wiry, or if I imagined all this the day he asked me to call him Robert instead of Bob. He is saying something about duty now, and I would ask to whom or what, but the ice cubes are crashing into the tray and any words of mine would only tumble and slide and be sucked away by the vacuum into which he speaks. And so I look out the window toward the Jemez Mountains, shrouded by summer clouds much too black for this early in the day, and remember that he is essentially kind, Brian loves him, and he still comes home to me each night. And perhaps someday we will leave, because he is also a man who is chased by discontent, a man who always wishes for the season opposite. I know this. I have been married to him for ninety-seven seasons.

I am no saint. Within a year after we moved to Los Alamos, he with his new doctorate in chemical engineering, I with my tired high school teaching certificate, his words began to sink below the level of my desire to hear, like steely marbles spilling out of his mouth and bouncing across the kitchen table, and me obliviously snapping at them with my fingernail until they shot off the edge, rolled around the chair legs, and came to rest in a silent heap at our feet. In that first year his voice changed from the many pitches of possibility to the quiet monotone of a man steeped in the murky culture of secrets that is Los Alamos National Laboratory. He could sketch for me the picture of his days only in vague silhouette, pencil drawings that could be easily erased or smudged, or painted away. His was a ghostly language of shape detached from place, a detailed description of shadow. Technical Area 50. I alternately pictured it pentagonal or changing form like a cumulus cloud floating somewhere above lab grounds. Was it next to a hexagonal TA-54 within a triangular Area G, did it have on it a metal outbuilding that was unbearably hot in summer, did anyone ever draw it on a map? Or perhaps it was less real, some nebulous ball of gas hovering above TA-35, or a soupy pit of barium 140, tritium, beryllium, and a thousand other ingredients, the names of which would spike his conversations like the bottle of sloe gin we tossed into the punch bowl at our high school prom. By the time he explained that TA-50 was a radioactive liquid treatment plant, into which flowed underground pipes streaming with radionuclides and chemicals from all across the lab's forty square miles, and out of which each year spilled eight million gallons of waste into Mortandad Canyon, I no longer cared.

But this morning his clothes cause me to care—steel-toed boots instead of black oxfords, worn jeans in place of navy chinos, faded blue work shirt replacing a crisp beige button-down, no tie. Every three months he spends his day collecting water and soil samples from a well near the bottom of the canyon, and every three months I spend my day picturing him cascading over the canyon ledge, or accidentally pitching himself into the wellhead and falling a thousand feet into a bottomless pool seething with uranium. And this morning I can add a lightning strike to his potential fate; the sky is darkening, the day seems in reverse. The sound of his boots in the hallway and the creak of the opening door mercifully call me back from the abyss, and I find myself admiring the muscle below his rolled-up sleeve as he carries his toolbox outside. He is leaving unusually early this morning, and kisses me as he wipes his brow and grumbles something about the swamp cooler not working in the high humidity. The season is always wrong.

Ephemeral. That is how Robert described the main drainage channel that once ran with water and carved Mortandad Canyon. Snowmelt and runoff flow through the upper canyon for a few days in spring, but the streambed is essentially dry, save the discharge from TA-50 which, Robert swore, was caught in three sediment traps near the bottom of the canyon and never left lab grounds. But that was before the Cerro Grande fire swept through our lives, up the canyon and into the mountain, before tall pines and thick brush that once held back mud and floods were turned to ash. Now the bare hills are covered in straw wattles, the stream banks with rock and wire mesh. Grass seed is glued to naked slopes, and fallen trees are stacked sideways, all to stop waters of some unknown season from rushing through a dry canyon stream, swallowing every strange molecule in its path, and breaking in waves across the ten miles southeast to San Ildefonso Pueblo, where it races toward the Rio Grande for purification—an impossible baptism of beryllium. Ephemeral, Robert says. I see him pause as he opens the car door. He turns around and I wave, but he is pointing at the Jemez, and we both cast our eyes toward the menacing darkness building above the mountain, the foothills where we camped each summer still bare and blackened from the fire.

Brian twists in his bed and moans softly in the next room, and I try to close the front door quietly so as to have an hour of peace. He will be

disappointed Robert left so early today but, really, that is too complicated a feeling for Brian to have. What he will miss is Robert patiently
undoing the knot of sheets that bunched around his ankles during the
night, rubbing his feet and legs as they dangle aimlessly over the side
of the bed, guiding him into his chair, taking him to the bathroom.
Brian is nineteen years old and loved, but I am no saint. Within five
months of his birth, and after countless meetings with neonatologists
and geneticists, I sat at breakfast one morning, looked out upon the
mountain, and told myself he should have been my third miscarriage
instead of our first child. There would be no playful swipes at colorful
mobiles above his crib, no first word, no wobbling on two feet at the
coffee table, our outstretched hands ready to catch him. There would
be no first step. Instead, there would be strangers in our home helping
him do what he would never do. And when he would sleep, we would sit
across the kitchen table late into the night planning not for some bright
boy's college tuition but for our son's most elementary care, committing
ourselves not to teaching him right from wrong, or how to ride a bike
or drive a car, but to outliving him. No, I am no saint. I cannot stand
that my son still drools. But I forgive my husband for the years of silent
blame, for believing that certain failures can only belong to a mother,
not to him, and not to strange substances that float on the air and seep
through the water of a small town he cannot leave. And I stay alive, and
keep my promise to my son.

My hour of solitude is reduced to twenty minutes, as a tremendous
clap of thunder wakes Brian. A severe thunderstorm warning flashes
across the bottom of the television screen, while Brian cries in the next
room. Just as I calm him, the phone rings. It is the young mother from
across the street, asking if I have looked out my window lately. She is
still new to this town, has not yet learned that the secrecy upon which
the lab stands is anchored by a privacy that permeates the whole town,
that you do not call your neighbor to discuss your children, or ask them
to look out the window. Instead, you attend the office Christmas party,
and send out a hundred Christmas cards. You say hello in the grocery

store, and wave at the man next door as you mow the lawn. And, while you send flowers and attend the crowded memorial service for a retired colleague of your husband, you never go to his widow's house afterward. My neighbor has learned nothing of this. She is talking about a tornado that hit her Texas town when she was ten years old, and something about her grandmother, as I cross to the window. I have lived here twenty-five years. It does not rain in the morning. The sky is as black as the day the town was evacuated during the fire.

Our neighborhood was spared that night, as we watched Los Alamos burn from the television in my sister's Santa Fe home. Robert had paced the living room for hours, his frantic eyes darting from the television to the picture window framing the orange glow in the northwest sky, his uneasy voice spilling into the cell phone pressed to his ear, fragments of conversation reverberating off the walls into our astounded silence. While he spoke of contaminated runoff, floods of some other season, I privately imagined an entire town in ash, the lab a pool of molten secrets, TA-50 nothing but a scrap of charred paper floating on a breeze, maybe just a stench left in the air. While Robert spoke of sediment traps and monitoring wells, of great waters coursing through the channels of Mortandad Canyon, I imagined a great exodus of the newly homeless and jobless, with me leading the way out. Instead, I found myself a month later in a Santa Fe bar with the new history teacher, checking my watch between glasses of wine, and sliding the candlestick in smooth, slow circles around our darkened corner table. And, while the one thing did not lead to the other, I spent the rest of that summer imagining waking each morning in his small adobe house nestled among the cottonwoods in Tesuque, while my fellow townspeople moved into FEMA trailers looking out upon the charred and barren slopes of the Jemez Mountains.

I am no saint, but neither is Robert a soldier. We have stayed for his career, sometimes we stayed just for money. We stayed because a promotion made TA-50 his, and him, the keeper of Mortandad Canyon. Then we stayed because of a fire that should have made anyone leave.

And now he says we stay to keep radioactive dust from the hands of a new enemy, that we are soldiers in some new war. "Hypocrite," I think, but do not say. "Some soldier you are, you whose father, proud member of that near-deified generation, bought your way into the National Guard while my brother and cousins slogged through mud up to their thighs and swatted at bloodsucking mosquitoes, Vietcong bullets flying mercifully past their heads and lodging in trees behind them, or maybe in heads of other boys. You're no soldier."

What I say, sardonically, is, "The only enemy you'll ever face, Robert, is a bad flood."

And now I would take it back, if I could. Rain has fallen in sheets all day, and it was hours ago when I last saw through the deluge to my neighbor's house across the street. She is probably hugging her two frightened children, making them sandwiches, maybe trying to call her mother in Texas. Water is rushing over the curb and stands halfway up our lawn. It moves toward the door, which is fighting the fiercest wind I have ever heard. Brian cried most of the day, and the lightning knocked out our electricity and telephone. As I snap fresh batteries into the radio, I notice the kitchen window is leaking. The water collects in small pools on the sill and cascades over the ledge, casting a shadowy stain onto the newly painted wall from last summer, and splashes to the floor in silent puddles around my feet. I light a candle and nervously move it in waxing circles about the kitchen table, and watch the flame's wavering reflection in the window. The dark has calmed Brian, and I am grateful for his company. He cannot picture Robert anywhere but here; he has never seen TA-50, or Mortandad Canyon with its traps and wells, or its ephemeral stream that empties into the Rio Grande.

It is ten o'clock. The radio announcer reported more than three hours ago that rescuers were searching for two men swept away in a flood in one of the canyons that cuts through the lab. There are eight such canyons, and I need not let my mind wander to any one in particular. The mudslides are clearly keeping many people from returning home on time tonight. When Robert finally pulls into our driveway, he will see the still-burning candle flickering in the kitchen window. He will walk through the open door, kiss me, and say, "Unbelievable!" After he removes his wet boots, he will peek into Brian's room and find him sleeping peacefully; he will quietly straighten the front wheels of Brian's chair, pull the blanket over his bare feet, and brush his hand lightly across his forehead. He will slowly shut Brian's door and tiptoe to our bedroom, where he will find the clean T-shirt, sweatpants, and socks I set out for him earlier this evening. The softness of the old cotton will feel warm against his chilled skin, and only then will he know how long this day has been, and how tired he has become. But his pace will quicken as he walks down the hallway and smells the black bean soup I made after the electricity came back on. And, as I fill the soup bowls and pour the glasses of wine, he will look out the window and talk about a cross-country ski trip next winter, still two seasons away.

My Fifteen Seconds of Flame

I T WAS SIXTEEN seconds, if you count that one second just before the engine exploded, that second when I thought I heard something and glanced out the window at the disappearing lights of Houston, glad to see them go, not yet knowing how desperately I would wish to see them again, right-side-up and from ground level. I am not sure I heard anything at all in that last, innocent second, other than perhaps the sound of my own life as it would never be again, a prelude composed of a blissfully ignorant breath and an unsuspecting heartbeat, performed in the one final moment before I would be forever changed, the rhythms that were me irretrievably altered, my atoms rearranged.

My first day of school was a critical failure, an unrehearsed debut on a stage without set marks, a fiasco of forgotten lines and unfocused lights. Unscripted and devoid of cues, I walked off on my own, with tightly curled hair, a blue and white dress, shiny new loafers, and a brown grocery bag stuffed with school supplies. I had no idea where my classroom was. After what seemed like an hour of wandering the halls in search of something I would not have even recognized, I walked home. My mother escorted me back, specifically to my room amid the stares of all my classmates. I made at least two more mistakes that first day. In late morning, the teacher scribbled something on the blackboard and asked for a volunteer to read it aloud. My hand shot up and I was promptly called upon. I had no idea what she had written on the board, and so I said nothing. Not a word. Then, in the middle of the afternoon, the bell rang and all the students ran outside and scattered onto the playground under the blazing, late August sun. Having never heard of recess, I walked home, my feet oozing blisters from my slightly oversized, new shoes. My mother thought I had probably had enough for the first day and did not make me return. There would be other days.

The right engine exploded in a flood of fuel and fire, racing past my window in the third to the last row and lighting the night sky for miles. Had anyone been watching from the darkness nearby, they could have seen my suddenly confused face at the window, lit up as well. But no one was there. Instead, I imagined a man in a rowboat on one of the lakes below, night fishing for walleye, lazily brushing the mosquitos from his face, his fluorescent line an eerie glow under the black light. From the corner of his eye he would notice the fireball in the sky, look up, and think, "Poor souls." He would be an elderly man, someone who had already seen it all, perhaps a veteran of the Battle of Midway. And now he was about to witness a group baptism in the quiet of his lake, a strange mixing of fuselage, fear, and fish. That is why he would just say of us, "Poor souls." I think I also imagined what we looked like from the vantage point of other planes in the area, the one that had taken off just before us, the two right after. Maybe, for just an instant, we were thought by some fellow traveler to be a newly discovered comet, a tailed sphere of fire in the distance, streaking across the night sky. But the pilots of those airplanes would have immediately radioed Houston air traffic control, and then instructed their crews to turn on the cabin lights as they quickly banked their jets away from us in an effort to spare their passengers a clear view of what was about to happen, what they would inevitably end up seeing all over tomorrow's newspapers and television stations. But some of the passengers would have already seen, with the clear vision that distance provides, what I was too confused to assimilate in that first second, what my eyes and ears had just taken in but what my brain had yet to name. Instead, while I was imagining a fisherman and other witnesses to what I could not yet witness for myself, all I could do was narrow my eyes, wrinkle my brow, and twist my face into a puzzled look.

I was in third grade when President Kennedy was murdered. Ask anyone what they were doing that day and they can tell you, in the most vivid and precise detail, even if they had only been a third-grader. I had walked home for lunch with my sister. When she and I opened the door my mother, practically shouting at us as though we had been the assassins, said, "Did you know the president was shot?!" I remember squinting my eyes and trying to recall if it was Washington or Lincoln who had been shot. I did not understand why she was asking this question, giving me this impromptu history test. But I suddenly remembered and answered, "I know, President Lincoln was shot at the theater; we learned it last year." He was dead, of course, by the time lunch ended and we had returned to school. I remember that Mrs. Halley was crying; she tried to read to us, and then told us to play quietly for the rest of the day, as she sat at her desk and stared out the window. I had never before seen an adult cry. But I also remember, just as clearly, that Mark Chavez showed us tricks with the red and blue yo-yo he had just received for his birthday, and that Amy Pierce and I practiced "Silent Night" for our duet in the Christmas program. That afternoon I played hopscotch on the sidewalk in front of our strangely quiet house and, for some reason, I remember that my mother had a doctor appointment. That was Friday. I do not remember much about Saturday, but on Sunday morning we were eating scrambled eggs when my father yelled from his chair in front of the television set, "They shot Oswald!" It must have been a confusing time for everyone.

Five more long and awful seconds passed before I fully realized what was happening. The plane had dropped abruptly at the moment of the explosion, and was now tipping to the right and falling backward. I could see the lights of Houston closing in from a suddenly strange perspective, which repulsed me and from which I had to immediately turn away. The fire continued to rip past my window as the fuselage shuddered and the nose struggled to reach skyward. I remember thinking we had hit a small airplane, since we were only a few minutes into our flight. As I recoiled from the fire just outside my window, what was left of my logic burst forth in a supremely illogical effort to take control. I looked at the floor and made sure my shoes were on, and that my purse was completely under the seat in front of me—that the path to nowhere was at least a clear path. I quickly tightened my seat belt, looked to see if the oxygen masks had been released, and recalled something about tucking my head to my knees. Instead, my feet suddenly lifted off the floor and my knees came nearly to my flinching face, which I was now protecting with my wildly gesturing hands, like an out-of-control mime in one last, desperate effort to tell a story to his unseeing audience. I and my suddenly awake companion and the teenaged boy next to her instinctively drew ourselves into reluctant fetal positions. The body wants to live, and it will raise its feet off the floor of a falling airplane just to have one more millisecond before any part of it slams into the ground. I guess we all hold tight for as long as we can, to whatever we think is ours.

The only bad year was seventh grade, that one strange year between child and teenager, that first year of junior high school when your worth is suddenly and without warning measured not by how smart you are, or how fast you can run, or how well you do the butterfly stroke but, instead, by the size of your breasts, which you measure on a daily basis, and by how easily you adjust to wearing pink frosted lipstick, acting demurely toward the boys (who seem no different than they were a few months ago in sixth grade), and crossing your legs like some archetypal lady whom you never meet but keep hearing about in the home economics class you swore you would never take, but which your mother made you register for anyway. You are no good at any of these things, not yet. Your home economics teacher cannot stand you because you crack your knuckles, forget to sit like the lady (but there are only girls in this class), and aspire to be the first female senator from New Mexico. But the real reason she dislikes you is that you are vehemently against the Vietnam War (which you are afraid your brothers will get killed in, since they are both over there, which she does not even know), and she knows if you were just a few years older she would probably be seeing you on the six o'clock news, some crazy, homosexual hippie rioting in the streets. And so you pretend to be sick as often as you can that year because, at least at home, you can still be you, at least for a while longer, and all you need is a little more time.

All those voices. Players in a discordant orchestra warming up, instruments out of tune, a cacophonous ritornello building to a screeching crescendo of terror. A gasp here, screams there, the man accustomed to commanding respect who, like a conductor thrusting his baton at an unwilling ensemble, conjured all the authority he ever had in his life, and in a booming voice simply yelled, "No!" Crying, I heard crying from somewhere nearby. Now I hear the woman behind me calling someone from her cell phone. She is talking quietly and her voice is shaking, and with all the other voices around me, for some reason I hear hers most clearly. "Pray for us, please. The plane is on fire..." And now I hear the sound of my own voice, as I turn and glance back at her through the gap between the seats. We are a symphony of strangers, now, in the ultimate private moment; I do not want this link to the living, I do not want some cell phone audience. Maybe I just do not want to pray yet. "No, not the cell phone." I sound like I am pleading; I have never pleaded in my life. "Oh please, hang up the phone." I say it twice. The man up front is shouting again, but all I can hear now is the multitude of voices, a loud tutti erupting into a roaring dissonance. People are contorted in their seats and twisting in all directions, and some are dancing with the wrong partners in this confusing choreography. The woman across the aisle and up one row is holding tight to the stranger in the maroon shirt beside her, while her husband alternately stares wide-eyed at the elderly couple across from him, then back at his wife. My companion and I are clutching each other, our feet still off the floor, but my right arm is reaching across her knees to grab the forearm of the teenaged boy who crouches in his seat beside her, and who tries to shield his eyes from the flames that are still so close to the window.

(It turned out the home economics teacher was partly right. When I was sixteen my best friend, Linda Morris, told me she was going to start spending more time with another girl. That was when I realized I was in love with her.)

―――――――

I now know how this story ends, though the author's meaning eludes me; my eyes have never been this open, my heart has never beaten this strong. I allow myself to quickly look out the window at the lights below, in order to measure the remainder of my life, to somehow quantify this terror. As the lone engine of the plane continues to struggle against gravity, I estimate my life expectancy to be reduced to about twenty seconds, but it could be shorter if the fire comes through the window. I turn back to my partner, but I no longer see her silver hair or smooth skin, the gracefulness of her hands. (I have forgotten what I look like.) Rather, I see straight past her glasses and beyond the brown of her eyes to a place filled with unimaginable fear. She says nothing at all. Not a word. My eyes mirror hers; we dare not blink, we barely breathe. I hear myself again. "Oh no," I am saying softly, to her as well as to myself, "Oh no." (I sound just like my grandmother in the days before her death, lying in her hospital bed repeating, like a fugue, "Oh dear.") I say it again, this time with a combination of resignation and the most profound sorrow I have ever known, as I contemplate our ending, our lives together nearly over. I briefly see our old calico and our house in Albuquerque, so much farther away now than just the physical miles that separate us, as my sorrow swells to unfathomable proportion, like the second movement of Schubert's Quartet in D Minor, or a devastating cello part just before the interlude. She kisses me, but our eyes remain frozen on each other as we hold fast for the end.

What I took away from the Linda Morris episode, other than the discovery of what it felt like to love someone and the strange fact that that someone happened to be female, was that I am not one who imprisons others; my bones are not proprietary, my flesh does not possess. I cried in the privacy of my bedroom, and was jealous of the other girl. But I kept it to myself and, even though I wanted to, I never asked her to come back to me, or said anything embarrassing, like, "Give me a second chance." And when my father was slowly dying many years later, when it was clear nothing more could be done for him, I never once asked God to spare his life, even though my sorrow, like his cancer cells, multiplied exponentially with each passing day.

Only fifteen seconds had passed since the engine exploded. My partner and I were still clinging to one another and had not yet noticed that the fire was out and the airplane was leveling again when, rising above the screaming and crying that still surrounded us, I heard the lone voice of the young man across the aisle yelling again and again, "It's okay! He has it under control! We're under control!" He shouted this three times above the noise before I and all the others could finally understand what he was saying. I allowed myself to look out the window again. The flames were gone, and the moon and stars were where they were supposed to be. But Houston was still a tense twenty minutes away. As the screams subsided, I let myself hear the steady sound of the one engine, sense the feel of being level again. I allowed myself to look for the airport runway, imagine a landing.

(For the first time that night I prayed, but I will forever wonder whether it was to a god who was mercifully with us, or completely and inexcusably absent.)

Continental had another plane ready within forty-five minutes, "...a bigger plane, a safe plane," the official said over the microphone to the third of us who were not in the bathrooms, or who had not already left the terminal, swearing to never fly again. Had I not been sleep-deprived from having been awake for nearly twenty-four hours, my day having begun on the other side of the Atlantic, I would never have boarded that plane. Instead, I think I shouted back, "The first plane was supposed to have been a safe plane, too!" We boarded anyway, those of us who were too exhausted to make different decisions, others who could joke about what the odds were of that happening again, as the new flight attendant crew greeted our much smaller group and prepared to serve the free drinks to which we were now all entitled. The teenaged boy who had been sitting next to my companion, and whose arm I had reached across for, took a seat in the empty row behind us, but not before smiling shyly as he passed by. Another man walked by and winked. He had approached me earlier in the terminal, as I lay pale and prostrate, and had said in a thick New Jersey accent, "It wasn't your day to go, hon; it just wasn't your day." The man in the maroon shirt took a seat across the aisle; the married couple whose wife had reached for him instead of her husband never re-boarded. I saw the young man walk past, the one who had broken through all the chaos to tell us we were under control again. (I will, with boundless gratitude, hear his voice shouting those words over and over for the rest of my life. The sound of his voice will resonate with me like a favorite song from my youth; for me, he will always be the sound of hope.)

Planes fly over the Rio Grande twice when they approach Albuquerque from the east, in order to land from the right direction. I have lived here all my life. Silver moonlight on that clear night reflected off the ribbon of river winding through the bosque. I do not know if the moon was nearly, or just recently, full. As we crossed the first time, my thoughts turned to my entire family living below, and I noticed that I had not once thought of them that night, nor had I called out for my dead father buried somewhere down there among the cottonwood trees. My life had not passed before my eyes; I was not summoned by the dead; no angel had tapped me on the shoulder. A woman with an eastern accent exclaimed to the man in the maroon shirt beside her, "That's the Rio Grande? It's so small. That's it?" I then heard him trying to explain the river, the dams and irrigation, the farmers and silvery minnows. "Everyone wants their piece of the river," he said. (Did he say piece or peace?) As we cross over the second time on our approach, all I can think of is that Paul Simon song "Peace Like a River." He was a solo act by then, and was probably singing about deeper waters, maybe the East River, or the Hudson as it spills into the harbor. The water below me runs less swift, is interrupted by sandbars. It is wound through thirsty fields, its course less direct. But one thing I know is that this river runs through my heart. What I do not yet know is that in one week I will buy a red Volkswagen Beetle with a CD player, a car that I can barely afford and in which I will listen again to Simon and Garfunkel, with the volume raised high, as I cruise on Saturdays to the swimming pool, the sun roof open, and the wind rushing through my salt-and-pepper hair.

The Inversion of Jeremy Jones

THE VIEW IS best understood from the bottom up. My back rests on a bed of blue grama and Indian ricegrass. A cool October breeze floats through the gorge, launches a willow leaf that swirls and flips and lands in the hair on my arm, whispers through the golden currant and gooseberry to my left, lifts my auburn hair against its natural part, lays it down again. My right leg dangles over the muddy bank of the Rio Grande, a school of rainbow trout swims past my bare foot. A lone blue heron pecks at some indistinguishable mass at the water's edge, but my eyes are fixed on a peregrine falcon circling overhead, as though it recognizes me from some other time.

"Aren't you Jeremy Jones?" The young woman in the bar had watched me from the corner table for over an hour. She and the single Budweiser she nursed seemed misplaced among the tables of tourists, sipping their margaritas, snapping their fingers at passing waitresses as beveled glasses grew empty. Taos is an uncomfortable mix of wealth worn on the sleeves of down parkas, or wrapped around necks heavy with turquoise and silver, and the kind of poverty that shivers in the cold after long days of serving enchiladas, or shoveling snow from the entries to ski lodges. And then there are the familiar fixtures like me, the singer in the bar next door. I alternate between the same two pairs of jeans each night and wear a long-sleeved, black shirt with mother-of-pearl buttons that match the inlay on the neck of my guitar. I roll up the sleeves to my elbows so women can notice the muscle and hair on my arms; my worn leather boots tap a steady cadence on the bottom rung of the stool. I sing about poor people, workers, and farmers, because that is what is expected of me. My songs belie a childhood of classical piano lessons in the upstairs conservatory of a Connecticut estate. By the time my last set ends, the remaining tourists are too drunk to notice that the old Jeep I climb into turns up a road opulent with summer houses built by money born of some other place.

"That's me," I said, tipping my Corona bottle her way. Two beers later I was huddled next to her in the dark corner, my knee brushing against hers. Her fingers, long and graceful, stroked the hair on my forearm as I peeled bills from my wallet for the next round. The light from the candle flickered across her pearlescent nails and reflected off eyes brown and soft. Before I knew it, my hand was filled with long, black hair, which I lifted off her face, held briefly to my nose, and placed over her shoulder.

I am paid with a cut of the door and tips from wealthy Texans wishing to impress their wives. But mostly I am paid in seduction. I am the sensitive musician, the poor minstrel. I spot a beautiful woman on a weekend trip with her girlfriends, and I sing to her. When she offers to buy me a drink after the first set, I shyly decline. She passes a creased napkin to me during the second set, on which is scrawled in unwieldy letters and ink bleeding to the edges, "I love your songs." But by now she thinks she loves me. I lower my eyes, and thank her. Her companions leave midway through the final set, whispering and smiling back at their friend who stays behind. "Do you know any Jackson Browne?" The words spill off her tongue, grown thick with drink, or maybe with just the hour. I finish with "Fountain of Sorrow," pack my guitar, coil the microphone cables, and humbly accept the cold beer she has set before me. By closing time, we are checking into the motel across the street, or slipping quietly through the lobby of the five-star hotel paid for by her husband, stuck in meetings in Dallas. When the night is through, she will know the touch of my breath upon her ear, the rough of my beard against her cheek. She will know my hands, my mouth, my flesh. When she wakes in the morning she will remember my smell. But she won't know where her poor musician has gone. She won't know that just before sunrise I turned up a road filled with the finest houses in Taos. Poor musicians don't live on my road.

But the woman with the Budweiser required no facade. She had just moved from southern Colorado, and stocked produce at Raley's. "I came in after my shift last night and heard you sing. I bet you've made a ton of CDs." I lied and said yes. A new persona suddenly emerged, dressed in my clothes, speaking in my voice—some spoiled musician who takes an impressionable girl to his home, pours her first flute of champagne, lowers the lights, burns the candles, lays her down upon sheets of silk.

It was just after two in the morning when we pulled into my driveway.

The wind spills over these canyon walls like a song sung from the inside out, a forlorn howl that is born in the heart, swells and pulses to the lungs where it's given breath, then rises like a phoenix from the throat. It flies spread-eagle over the tops of Rocky Mountain juniper and piñon pine, harmonizes with the cries of a startled bobcat, a gray fox. It ricochets like a bullet against great lava boulders that hide nesting habitats of osprey and red-tailed hawks. A peregrine falcon shudders, opens its wings, and reluctantly takes to the night in great circles toward the ground.

I never saw the two men behind the carport, never heard their footsteps as they followed us to the front door, or smelled the cigarettes on their breath. I drove right past the green Neon parked at the bottom of the hill but failed to see it, failed to remember it driving slowly down my street just a few days earlier. I only felt a powerful shove against my back as I turned the key. The door closed quickly behind me, filling my house with a cold wind and bringing with it not two but three strangers. I heard the woman's whispers, then her laughter, the sound of seduction coming to an abrupt end.

The barrel of the gun was sharp against the back of my neck. I compliantly led them to my study and unlocked the drawer that held my credit cards, my checks. "Take whatever you want," I said calmly, as though offering them a tray of hors d'oeuvres. "My wallet's in my back pocket," I volunteered. My heart beat strong against my chest; my voice did not falter. I strode past silver vases that had sailed from England with my great-grandmother, paintings that had adorned limestone walls of a Sheffield manor house, to be hung a lifetime later in a Connecticut estate, and then upon these four walls. My boots sank deep into ornate carpets sculpted in Persia, my fingers brushed across spines of rare first editions I promised my grandmother I would someday read. "This is all worth a lot, just take it; take my Jeep." The last thing I offered was my guitar. By then my palms were sweaty.

"Shut up. You're taking us to the ATM."

"I'll just give you my number. Look, it's on a scrap of paper in my wallet that shows a phone number for Aunt Marilyn; it's the last four digits."

"Shut up, asshole."

The four of us climbed into the Jeep. They made me drive. We cruised the streets of Taos, emptied of its people, and turned corners I had never before taken as the Jeep filled with the acrid smoke of crack cocaine, only to end up again at the bottom of my street.

"Slow down. Pull up next to the Neon."

The woman and one of the men got into the green Dodge, then followed us five miles north to the parking lot of a bank in El Prado. I walked up to the ATM alone. It was cold and I needed to pee. I forgot my PIN, and had to return to the Jeep and ask one of the men to look at the piece of paper in my wallet. "Aunt Marilyn, 737-0813." I withdrew the highest amount allowed.

"Please, just take the money and my Jeep, and leave me here," I said in a strangely polite voice. But they made me drive on, heading west out of town on U.S. 64.

Some days are better lived in reverse, their hours capsized, their events turned upside-down in a tumbling vertigo. The toe of my left boot is scuffed and stained with western wheatgrass. It is separated from its sole, a clump of broom snakeweed protrudes from the gash in the leather. I missed the river by just a foot; it moves past me now, gurgling over stones that mock this failed baptism. Bits of sagebrush dot my torn jeans. A jackrabbit races across the open mesa, a coyote cries in the night.

I turned forty this year, the same age as the bridge that spans the Rio Grande Gorge. Some mother loved me, but I don't recall when. The Jeep's headlights reflected off the steel I-beam of the approach, and the deck rattled as we drove west across its quarter-mile span. Just as I wondered if it would be the final bridge I crossed, the impassive voice next to me said, "Pull into the lot." The last thing I saw before turning off the lights was a sign that read Persons Throwing Objects Off Bridge May Be Prosecuted. Someone laughed, and it might have been me. The green Neon parked alongside us, and the second man got out. By now I had forgotten the woman's face, the feel of her hair in my unknowing hands. I couldn't remember what I looked like. My name was slipping from memory, like ice melting through fingertips.

Nerves fired randomly, cells multiplied in alarm, atoms rearranged. My senses vanished like a specter into the night, as we walked back toward the center of the bridge. I heard a panicked man talking about cash and a Jeep, guitars and credit cards, but my ears did not recognize the voice as mine. I smelled urine, but didn't feel the wet warmth as it made its way down my leg. I swear I closed my eyes, yet I remember the moon. It was nearly full, and I could see in the distance the silhouette of the Sangre de Cristo Mountains north of Taos, a colossal backdrop to the mesa that stretched before me. I have stood here before. My father once held my trembling hand upon this mighty crossing of steel and concrete, and assured me it was built to outlive the flesh and bones to which it gave passage.

A second moon suddenly enveloped the night. It reflected off the railing, cast a garish light on the canyon walls, illuminated the snake of a river six hundred feet below.

Some stories are best told from finish to start. My Jeep is parked in the rest area at the end of the bridge, but there is no sign of me. Some say the ghost of a young woman haunts this place, urging all she comes upon to jump. Know this. I did not fall; I did not jump. The muscles of my arms stayed firm and never gave way. The fingers of my left hand pressed hard over the top of the railing, as if playing a bar chord on a beloved guitar. I held on with all I had until the last of me was pried from the cold steel of the bridge. Know this. I never cried; I never screamed. In my silence, and halfway down at three hundred feet, I found grace. Or maybe grace found me, and delivered my heart gentle to the ground.

September Light

Switch off the lamp at the top of the stairway, as dusk calls you to the armchair at your window, just fifty yards from a weathered cottage across a grassy hill. Peer through the gap in your lace curtains as your tired eyes reach for the old cabin, and picture not an ordinary man from six hours ago, tall and slender, slightly bent at the shoulders, silver hair reflecting the midday sun burning above Puget Sound, but the man's silhouette through a small window divided by four panes, backlit by a second small window that looks upon the Sound behind him. He is no longer ordinary. Sandwiched between the two windows in this waning light, he becomes a caricature of himself, a monolithic shadow moving in the slowest of gestures, the opening of a cabinet, the reach for what can now be seen as a wine glass, a pour, and then a pause before taking the glass to his lips and arching his neck slowly backward as he drinks.

Cast your eyes left, as though to the previous frame of a child's picture book, and see through a larger window the silhouette of an easel, the canvas cloaked in the growing dark, its image withheld. He prefers his canvas large, his stroke broad. Feel the stem of the goblet rotate slowly between your fingers, as you sit perched in your own darkness and wonder whether he still wears the faded jeans and blue work shirt from earlier in the day, if the sleeves remain rolled up, revealing arms once strong, now flaccid with the years and spotted with age. Take wine to your own lips, and watch him as he crosses from the one frame into the other, and slowly back again.

Consider whether he will take the brush into his waiting hand.

He nearly saw you today at the market on Water Street, but you slipped like a specter into the next aisle. Perhaps he will bake the halibut he bought there, steam the asparagus. Or maybe he will just finish his bottle of wine and slip out of view as he did the night before, the brief glow through the fogged bathroom window a garish spotlight cast upon another day of failed intentions. Was his lunch of fish and chips and cold beer enough to sustain him? It is hard to know. He sat at the long cedar bar of Gleason's Ale House until nearly three, picking at his food like a tired hound, the stool creaking like an old wooden boat moored too close to its dock.

"Another cold one for you, Erich?" The barkeeper reached for a rag and wiped down the counter, sticky with salt and bread crumbs and mug rings of lager left by old men who had sat hunched upon those stools, and had since moved back into the wandering streets, up the hills home, or toward the pier to watch the ferries come and go. Men too old to notice a table tucked away in a corner.

Remember his voice as he peeled dollar bills from the tarnished money clip he keeps in his right jeans pocket, and replied, "Thank you, no. I'd best be getting back to it."

His is a voice steeped in time, a voice that traveled across an ocean, and found its home two thousand miles east of the continent's edge from which it now speaks, a voice without place. Hear him again. He seems to speak to his waiting canvas now. His arms loom large above the easel, the left hand clutching the wine glass, the right frozen in an imploring gesture. Strain to see him, as the distance between you recedes into darkness.

Imagine what you cannot see.

The light over the bathroom mirror spreads a pall across his skin, makes him grayer than he is. For a moment he sees himself standing off to the side, just a boy eye level to his father's chest, looking up to the mirror and watching the rhythmic scraping of the razor traverse Karl Huber's coarse face, covered in thick shaving soap from the dark, chipped mug that rolled out of Hamburg's central train station in 1947, packed carefully alongside his mother's enamel kettle and his own leather *völkerball*, across marshlands and dunes shrouded in autumn fog toward the harbor on the Elbe's North Sea outlet and a steamship waiting to take it to America. The same chipped mug from which three neighbors, secreted away in 1941 in a makeshift compartment below Karl Huber's press, had shared cold milk that came daily around the corner from the icebox outside Karl Huber's apartment. Among them was a beautiful woman called Clara with whom, during ten nights of firestorms that drove Erich and his mother deep into tunnels below Hamburg's streets, Karl had taken comfort, only to lose her in the confusion that was the war's end.

Erich Huber blinks, looks back to the mirror, taller now, but still slight of build, his blue eyes nearing gray, sunken and set deep in hollows beneath his creased forehead, straight brown hair gone thin and silver, like wire, his seventy years staring back at him as he splashes cool water upon his face.

A brown leather wallet, worn and discolored, lies open and flat upon the bureau as he fishes through the top drawer for a clean T-shirt. An aging man stares out from the driver's license behind the plastic on the left side of the wallet, opposite this a snapshot of a young woman. The photograph is tattered from touching, the finish tired, colors fading. Sometimes he stops at this point, considers her face. Sometimes he wonders if she has watched him age in the darkness of this wallet.

Her hair is black, long. It is parted just left of center and pulled behind her ears, only to appear again cascading in pendulous waves over the front of her bare shoulders. It was early September, but very bright that day. Had the photograph been taken just a bit earlier, had the backlight been only slightly different, there would have been a touch of summer red toward the hair tips. In stark contrast to the hair is the pale of her face, her arms. She had the whitest skin. Her eyes are dark blue, set deep beneath thick brows. There she is, looking at something just beyond his shoulder, her red lips easing into a shy trace of a smile. Her left hand is balanced lightly on the railing of the old hickory footbridge, Moss Creek washing over stones below. In the field behind her are the first of autumn blooms—the yellow panicle of goldenrod, black-eyed Susan, gentian as blue as her eyes, Queen Anne's lace as white as her skin.

There she is, from a time just hours before he first made love to her. A week later he brought her to meet his parents. The girl's surname meant nothing to Karl. But her mother's story spilled over her lips and crashed onto the kitchen table like the clatter of fine china as it slips out of trembling hands and hits the floor.

"My mother spent the war hidden under a trapdoor below a printer's press in Hamburg, along with two of her neighbors. Each day the printer would pass down milk in an old, chipped mug. When he could, he would bring a chunk of bread, sometimes an apple. I never knew my real father. He was lost to the camps."

It was Clara's story. In search of displaced friends, she and her daughter had made their way across the Atlantic, and then into the Ohio valley just a few miles up Moss Creek, where she married a mill worker from Frankfurt, only to be widowed a year later. Karl Huber's face went ashen as he stared across the table into the eyes of his daughter.

Two days later he stood at Clara's apartment door, her beauty still radiating across the years, his hands still bearing ink stains from a press that was her salvation. They spoke in hushed tones of comforts taken during nights of bombings, of common journeys, and innocent children colliding on improbable paths. They spoke of roadblocks to be set, and passages denied. Karl handed her an envelope filled with cash, and she and her daughter left the next week. Erich Huber knocked on their door for a month, peeked through the gap between pulled curtains, tried to make sense of a room emptied of its people, its possessions, as the miles between them gathered like thunderheads on a hot, August afternoon.

And now what of this distance, these fifty yards? The light from his bedroom meets you halfway. Soon it will expire, be lost to this night. Fifty yards. Down the rickety stairs, a quick pause in front of the mirror, a wrinkled hand smoothing white hair, a touch of red lipstick, then quietly out the door and up a grassy hill. The outside air is warmer than expected, the slope of the hill gentler. A sudden illumination above the easel draws your eye inside, as he takes the brush to his hand.

Fifty yards. You have been this close. Once you stood in the dark outside a screened porch, as the glow from a television cast uneven shadows across living room walls, and flashes of light upon his sleeping face. The next day you imagined yourself comforting him at the side of an open grave as he buried Karl Huber, instead of watching from a stand of oak trees on a sultry day, mosquitoes swarming just beyond the veil that hid your face. Fifty yards. Just two years ago, told by neighbors he had moved west, you drove across the country and found him in a bar in Taos, running his finger in slow circles around the burgundy-stained rim of a crystal goblet, while another man two seats down from you spun an old pocketknife on the sticky bar. Some musician was singing "Fountain of Sorrow" to an adoring, drunk woman.

The next day you followed him to the east end of the bridge that crosses the Rio Grande Gorge, taking care to keep several car lengths behind. He walked to the center of the bridge and stood for what seemed a lifetime, looking down upon gooseberry and red-tailed hawks and rushing waters six hundred feet below. You could no longer help yourself. You walked onto the bridge, surreptitiously took his picture, then waited in your car for him to leave. The man from the bar who had been spinning his pocketknife was parked in the truck next to you. He watched, as you wiped away your tears.

Fifty yards. The space between you reduced to this. Walk to where the light from the easel touches your feet; consider his subject. The lamp reveals a canvas filled with a still faceless woman with long black hair, her hand at rest upon some old railing, a field of flowers in the background. He has painted you a hundred times, always in September light.

Stand at his door.

Fifty yards, all behind you now. A distance as arbitrary as the two thousand miles and forty years that preceded this night. For what purpose now, why at this late hour? All the children never born have long been saved. The faces of those who would remember lie rotting in graves overgrown with weeds, or in dark forests across an ocean. Moss Creek, diverted through a concrete channel to make way for a shopping mall, runs now only in the hearts of those who ever sat on her banks, and let her cool waters rush over their intertwined feet in a baptism of desire.

Feel the steadiness of your hand as you knock on his door.

Your mother once spoke of optimal distance, that virtuous space between any two hearts—a teacher and his student, friends, a brother and sister. An idea meant for comfort, now grown tired with the years, an idea too small to hold innocent desires born along creeks on warm September days. The distance was never optimal, and for this you were never sorry. It spreads itself before you now, taunting, as it always has, an empty canvas yearning to be covered in bold images, thick paints bleeding to the edges, a cacophony of color. It asks for a bridge, not monumental in stature, not suspended from mighty towers or spanning vast horizons. It asks not at this late hour for some feat of engineering, but rather for simple crossing, not unlike a narrow footbridge of aged hickory and worn handrails. It asks to be closed.

Hear his footsteps grow near. Listen for the turning of the knob; see the light as it makes its way across the threshold.

Texas Armadillo

THIRTY-FIVE YEARS AGO I drove this road wearing nothing but worn leather sandals, the sweet smoke of a smoldering joint rising like a specter from the stuffed ashtray, drifting past the cracked dashboard and vanishing through the open window of my '61 turquoise Corvair, my girlfriend pressed up against me and laughing so hard the flowing, auburn curls spilled over her face and cascaded in waves down her tremulous back, her screams a raucous counterpoint to Janis Joplin's "Piece of My Heart." It was the month before I went to Vietnam. I had one hand on the wheel and the other on her knee, and we were going so fast when we crossed the Pecos we hardly noticed it ran with water.

Now I wear a tattered Albuquerque High T-shirt over a baggy pair of blue sweats, and faded sneakers. I lean forward and my stiff fingers grip the wheel tight as another semitruck whizzes by, rocking the minivan like a Texas tornado. Jesus, I look just like my father. My wife changes the CD to Nanci Griffith and says something out the window about the river being dry as the Rio Grande back at El Paso. That was nearly five hours ago, and I remember thinking it was so dry that all that reflected the sunlight was the barbed wire rising above its north bank, but I say nothing. Another truck passes, choking us in a baptism of dust, and I realize I've been counting dead deer for half an hour and doubting if any are left alive in the entire state of Texas. I flash on my baby sister in her crib, a spot of mud on her forehead, dead as those deer.

My breath goes slowly free as the rearview mirror reflects an empty road, and I wonder how long Laura's hand has been on my knee. Just then I see a red convertible approaching fast ("like a bat out of hell," my father would say). The large flag attached to the antenna is suspended like a swollen wind sock. It snaps like a shot in the distance, as the car thunders by. The pair in the car are wearing matching red shirts. The driver's left hand is loose over the wheel, the other on the arm of the woman next to him, diamond rings flashing like steelies upon her pudgy fingers, her mouth agape in laughter. The tag says Florida, but the shape of the driver's eyes says Southeast Asia. An armadillo grazes on some switchgrass at the side of the road, bald and ugly and having more plates on its head than the one left in my platoon leader's by Charlie ("lie still in your trench and play dead," my father had said). I wonder what the hell it's doing out of its burrow in the middle of the day, but at least it's alive. My fingers pause only slightly as they brush across my wife's arm on the way toward the glove compartment. The walnut grips of the Colt Python .357 Magnum fill my steady hand, and I accelerate.

Where the Dead Man Lives

THE BODY OF an average man contains a little more than five quarts of blood. But a dam can burst and a river suddenly change course when a decidedly unaverage man, one who not only suffers sadness but who is inhabited by it, looks over his shoulder in the middle of some night and sees the shadow of his own solitude gaining on him fast. Compounding his distress is the sound of disappointment he hears marching across his years, mocking him with a steadily growing cadence, becoming cacophonous, then deafening. In the silence he implodes, places a razor blade to his neck, and makes a quarter-inch cut in his large carotid artery, causing all those quarts of blood to shoot out of him and spray onto the walls and floor at whatever position he last lost consciousness.

Though others will later say, for dramatic or other effect, "He slit his own throat," the injury is more a nick than the gaping wound that such a phrase conjures. This is the implosion of a precise man, a gentle man. He feels for his pulse and makes the cut. It is on the right side of his neck under the jawbone, and is only a quarter-inch deep and less than an inch long. He hardly feels the pain of the blade. Instead, all in the matter of a second he feels the wetness jump with a spurt at the mirror and then move with lightning-fast speed down his bare chest, all the while spraying red at a velocity in excess of nine feet per second on whatever is in the path of his still moving body. He steps from the bathroom, so quickly that he never really sees in the mirror what he has done. But he knows. The blade drops into the sink with a slight, clinking sound of metal upon metal that he never completely hears.

Two, maybe three steps and he is at the top of the stairs, his skin already cold and sweaty, his breaths deep and rapid as his heart tries to preserve blood flow to his suddenly confused brain. His pupils are dilated now, and a lightheadedness beyond that caused by the vodka drunk earlier begins to take him away. He half falls, half sets himself down on the pillow he had moments earlier placed above the top step, his head to the side and falling toward the second step, his arms clutching his chest, knees bent toward his waist. He is naked, his final posture an impassive fetal position.

He feels a strange suction in his head now and is suddenly asleep, just over two minutes after making the cut. But his body still contains a few more quarts and he still has a hole in his neck. His heart keeps pumping his blood to the opening in his carotid until there is not enough left to pump, and then his heart stops and he dies, without even knowing, at the top of the stairs. It is almost twenty minutes since he cut himself. But his five quarts of blood continue slowly streaming down the steps for another hour and a half, gathering in a slowly spreading pool at the bottom of the stairs.

He never dreams it will look like this; he never intends for the finding to be so awful.

Several hours ago he is a living man. He breathes, he is mobile. But this is a quiet house around which he paces, the silence broken only by the sounds of his shuffling feet and the occasional crackling noises emanating from somewhere within the walls, as though wooden floors sense this troubled walk. He pours himself another vodka, straight up but still drinking from a glass. He is of average height and slender, strong build, his skin dark like the kind grandmother he recalls from childhood. For a transitory moment he conjures the old woman, sees her smile as she waves at him from the front porch of the house in Las Cruces. He is ten and rides his bike in circles just beyond the steps where she sits. This is where the night could have turned out differently; instead, his thoughts turn back on himself and he feels again the pulsing of his sorrow. He stands before the mirror in the entryway and sees his silver hair, straight and thick, the dark of his eyes, sharp features, his own handsomeness still hanging on in spite of the lateness of his middle age. But on this night the mirror only absorbs what is placed before it, little is reflected back. He averts his eyes from the image of himself and moves away.

He is standing at the living room window now. It has been night for hours, and he sees the streetlight reflecting off the surface of the irrigation ditch that runs along the front of his property, and that once brought water to the fields where his and all his neighbors' houses now stand. Near the end of every March, the ditch riders open the headgates to the mother *acequia* and her lateral *sangrías* and, for the next seven months, make the Rio Grande traverse a foreign path through the dirt and concrete ditches that snake through the North Valley where he lives. It is late October, but the water still runs. In front of a quarter moon stand the silhouettes of two river cottonwoods, forty years older than the new lawn he planted last spring and through which their trunks now protrude. The streetlight catches the stained glass next to the front door, and sends refracted beams of alternating yellow and green light that travel from the surface of the bistro table down to the chrome legs of the chairs. He unlocks the door.

He walks to the kitchen, to the uncharacteristic mess that it is. All around him he sees remnants of meals prepared, but uneaten. He grabs the vodka bottle, turns out the light, and moves to the study down the hall. His gait grows less steady and he hears himself laugh as he falls against the bookcase, sending dusty law school treatises and green hornbooks crashing to the floor. When a solitary man's laugh turns derisive, the contempt is for himself. He knows he has turned some kind of corner in this night. He drinks from the bottle now. The client files on his desk have fallen to the floor and are spilling their papers around the chair legs; quickly and without looking back he leaves the room. He walks past the guest bedroom without even a glance, as his eyes turn up toward the second-floor landing.

The stairs grow harder to climb, and he bounces from wall to banister until finally he is at the top, where he stumbles into his room and falls into the unmade Italian platform bed. He takes a last gulp of vodka, spilling most of it on his shirt, and manages to set the bottle onto his nightstand. The digital clock reads 3:32. He stands now, stumbling, and somehow removes all his clothes, dropping them in small, rumpled piles on the bedroom floor and across the landing along his way to the bathroom. This night is like a vacuum now, and he feels on his skin and in his chest the suction of unnamed sorrows, obscure disappointments. He opens the medicine cabinet and takes the shaver and, fumbling, removes the blade as he walks back into the bedroom. He sits on the edge of his bed and without any hesitation makes a cut across his left wrist, and then another. But nothing happens; his cuts are shallow and run perpendicular instead of parallel to the vein. He has made barely a scratch and passes out backward onto the bed, his neck pressed at an awkward angle against the white leather headboard.

He wakes in a couple of hours and turns his head to the window. The first sign of light is coming into the eastern sky, but it brings no solace, raises no hopes. Consolation has been discarded, or maybe just lost, along the side of some levee path taken too many turns and too much time ago. This man knows no comfort. He rises, walks to the bathroom, and urinates. His sleep has given him back his steady feet. He sits on the edge of the bathtub under the brightness of the heatlamp, staring at the floor and listening to the sound of his own breathing. A few minutes later he abruptly stands and brushes his teeth. He returns to the bedroom and retrieves the blade and pillow. As he walks back to the bathroom, he sets the pillow at the top of the stairs. He stands at the mirror and makes his cut. He has been awake for just over six minutes. His phone will ring at 7:00 this morning, and he will be found just after 7:30.

Douglas Anthony Mondragon, so much in a name. A quiet decision on a winter night between his expectant parents, his own father's first name, the grandfather he never knew for his middle name. So much in a name. A birth certificate, and then baptism and report cards, confirmation and diplomas. What his grandmother shouted out the door on summer evenings when it was time for supper, and he was nowhere in sight. So much in a name.

His secretary and an associate found him. The unlocked front door, the missed early morning meeting. He knew who would come for him, who would not. His five quarts of blood still trickled down the stairs to the pool at the bottom where Sara Carter and Jacqueline Graham stood, hearts racing, eyes wide. The blood was fresh and still moving; motion is life, thought Jacqueline. And the eyes were half open, gaze fixed upon them at the bottom of the stairs. Doug, Doug?

The police arrived within minutes of Sara's call. By then, she and Jacqueline were standing silent in the morning sun outside Douglas Mondragon's open front door. Two Albuquerque officers ran inside, while a third took the women out to the street by his squad car and fired questions they would never remember. ("Which of you called 911, who is he, who are you, how did you get in?") The siren of the approaching ambulance added to the confusion of the morning, as the women struggled to explain what appeared to them inexplicable.

Inside, the officers quickly determined that this was an empty house. They didn't bother checking for a pulse; it was clear there was nothing left to pump through this man's body. They quietly commented on his state of nakedness, the three-foot replica of the *Statue of David* in the entryway, the series of paintings of the male lovers in the living room, posters on the landing wall. One radioed in the code for a possible homicide, and a request for crime scene technicians and the medical examiner. They had not yet seen the razor blade in the sink.

The ambulance came and left quickly, empty; Doug was not to be saved. One of the officers who was first into the house came out to the street where Sara and Jacqueline were, and asked if there had been signs he was suicidal. They had found the razor blade in the sink. Before the women had a chance to answer, the interviewing officer interrupted. "He had been acting strangely over the past few weeks, they said, coming in late to work or calling in sick, smelling of alcohol one day, didn't even call in yesterday, missed a meeting this morning, completely out of character." The other officer asked the women if they knew anything else. They didn't. As they started to cross the street to Sara's car, Jacqueline turned back and said, "His parents and sister are in Las Cruces, but he has a brother who works for a local contractor. I think it's Connally Brothers Construction, or something like that."

Two field workers from the Office of the Medical Examiner arrived in a dark blue van. They carried matching duffel bags to the front door, where they put on latex gloves and green, plastic coveralls. They stopped on the porch under the latillas and snapped plastic coverings over their shoes, masks over their faces, and cameras around their necks. A technician knelt over Doug Mondragon. He gently brushed Doug's hair onto a piece of wax paper, rolled a tape pad over his skin, lifted his fingerprints, and collected his blood. By late morning the technician was done. He wrapped Doug in a sheet while the woman retrieved the gurney from the van. They placed him in a body bag, and the dark blue van slowly pulled away.

(The final autopsy report was issued six weeks later. It said that the identity of the decedent was established by circumstances of death and discovery of the body, and that the general appearance of the body was that of a well-nourished white male who appeared to be the stated age of fifty-nine years. It described his height in inches and his weight in pounds, that his limbs were symmetrical and his head normally shaped, that his internal organs were properly placed and of their proper respective weights. No part of him defied description. The report noted the presence of an especially high percentage of ethanol in his blood. The manner of death was identified as suicide, the cause exsanguination.)

The police chaplain had yet to make his calls by the time Sara and Jacqueline returned to work and told the others in the office, the receptionist and the bookkeeper. "The blood was everywhere," said Sara. She spared no details, as the receptionist cried and the bookkeeper turned pale. She then called the two senior partners, Pete Rivera and Bernadette Williams, a brother and sister team who were on vacation with their spouses in California. "Doug's dead," she said. "He slit his own throat." Bernadette felt a burst of adrenaline as she momentarily flashed back to the unusually sentimental goodbye Doug had given her as she had left for vacation. Just as quickly, she regained herself and asked for the telephone number of the brother's construction company. She reached the foreman, who said he would find Doug's brother and tell him. Bernadette also called directory assistance for the number of Doug's parents in Las Cruces. She called and told Doug Mondragon's father. The chaplain, not knowing these calls had already been made, found Doug's brother at the construction site as he was gathering his things. "I already heard," Doug's brother said. "I'll call my parents."

A few hours later the last of the police officers shut Doug's door and released the scene to Doug's brother. Blood was still all over the house. It remained there for another day, until a professional cleaning service was shown in by Doug's brother, and two hours later, two cleaning women carried the mess away in open laundry bags stained and brimming with reddish-brown, saturated towels containing approximately five quarts of blood. A few minutes later two young boys would ride past the house on their bicycles, and one would point to the house and say, "That's where the dead man lives." By then, Bernadette and Pete would be standing in Doug's front yard with Doug's brother. They wouldn't know what else to do.

For many months, Jacqueline would worry about the role she might have played—that maybe she could have stopped him. All those clues, she'd say. He'd been behaving terribly for the past six months, so out of character. He made her attend a seminar on copyright law, and then he brought her in on all his cases. And the strange questions he had asked her. "I've got another friend with AIDS. He's really bad off. Can his sister get his house without a lot of trouble if he doesn't have a will? His parents wouldn't be any problem." She answers, thinking this is a surprisingly naive question coming from him, and three weeks later he asks her to do a will for him. "Don't you want a living will and power of attorney, too?" He doesn't. He leaves his house to his sister.

In the week after the memorial service, Sara would say that his handwriting had become very sloppy just a couple of weeks earlier, that she had to keep going into his office and asking what this word and that word were, that the bookkeeper even had to verify his initials "DAM" on his time sheets. Not too long ago, she smelled alcohol on his breath after lunch one day. Completely out of character. And then he just walked out last Tuesday in the middle of the afternoon, didn't even say he was going for the day. Sara takes another job in less than three months.

The receptionist would cry almost every day for a week after the memorial service. She has a few photographs of Doug from various office social functions over the years, a Christmas party, a picnic. She'd like to have one enlarged, framed, and hung high on the wall in the reception area. Bernadette Williams and Pete Rivera say no, they don't think that would be a good idea. A few weeks later she gives everyone in the office a five-by-seven photograph of Doug, so they can all remember him. She leaves just a couple of months after Sara does.

Jacqueline would one day let go of her belief that she might have possessed the power to have altered this course of events, or that she could have gained as a friend in death one whom she had called merely an acquaintance in life. But while handling his probate, Jacqueline had seen a clearer picture of Doug, had come to know him a little better. She saw his bank account balances, his credit card debt, that he liked books and nice restaurants, cash on hand. That he had a round-trip plane ticket to Chicago for the week after he died. Was this a small hesitation, had he considered another way out? The possibility of Doug having had a second thought would cause Jacqueline to feel a sickness in the pit of her stomach long after she stopped thinking of him.

For the first few weeks after Doug's death, though, Jacqueline's eyes passed right over amid his desk clutter a two-by-three-inch yellow Post-it note stuck to the desktop, which read in his shaky handwriting "DAM—sad scenarios." By then, it had already been authoritatively stated that he had left no note. She wouldn't ever know exactly when he wrote it, or exactly what he was thinking. But she decided that it was his suicide note, and that she was not the proper person to have it. Instead, Jacqueline showed it to Sara, who didn't necessarily agree that it was his suicide note. She persuaded Sara to call Doug's sister anyway, who also agreed it wasn't necessarily anything and that, no, nobody in her family would want it. So Jacqueline, a most unlikely recipient, became the keeper of Doug's note, and stuck it to the back of the picture the receptionist had given her.

The measure of an average man can be taken by his affinities. A different kind of man, though, a man with a dearth of connection, a paucity of attachment, ends up being measured by strangers. But not before he enters the world altogether tethered to a mother's blood, wholly dependent on a father's goodwill. A brother and then a sister, the rest of a life. Community awaits him.

Doug had already been removed by the dark blue van and admitted to the county morgue by the time Greg Mondragon's foreman asked him to come into the office trailer, and said in an uncharacteristically quiet voice, "Greg, someone from your brother's office called. Anyway, I don't quite know how to put this to you, but she says he's apparently been found...at his house. I really don't know anything about this or, you know, even if it's true, for that matter. She sounded pretty upset. Anyway, you maybe better get your stuff and head on out of here, find out what's what."

Greg's heart began to pound and he was just trying to think straight. It was probably Bernadette who called; no, she and Pete are out of town.

He doesn't know anyone else to call at Doug's office. He'll call his parents. No, calm down. He'll just go over to Doug's house and find out what, if anything, is going on. Greg was rushing around gathering his jacket and thermos, and taking off his tool belt, when the chaplain from the police department approached him and said that his brother was dead and that the cause appeared to have been suicide (Greg won't ever remember the chaplain's exact words). "I already heard," Greg said. "I'll call my parents."

Doug's father answered. There was a pause after Greg broke the news, followed by a barely audible and defeated sounding "Oh...oh" on the other end of the line. And then, in words he would immediately consign to a place where memory doesn't live, Doug's father told Mrs. Mondragon, whose face turned red and whose eyes flashed with anger. "Call Melissa," was all she said.

An obituary ran in the Friday and Saturday evening papers, which read, "Douglas A. Mondragon died on Thursday, October 27, at the age of 59. He is survived by his parents, Douglas T. and Rose Mondragon, brother Gregory Mondragon and family, and sister Melissa, and her daughter and fiancé, all of Las Cruces, as well as by several aunts, uncles, and cousins. Douglas was an attorney in Albuquerque. A memorial service will be held on Sunday at 1:00 P.M. in the chapel of McMurphey's Funeral Home, 135 San Lorenzo NE."

(What Doug's parents never knew is how angry this obituary made Bernadette, and that she and Pete arranged for a second obituary, which read, "Douglas A. Mondragon, prominent Albuquerque attorney and partner in the firm of Rivera, Williams and Mondragon, died at his home on October 27. He was 59. Doug was born in Las Cruces and graduated from St. John's High School, where he lettered in football and cross-country track and was a member of the Spanish Club, speech team, and National Honor Society. Upon graduation, Doug took a scholarship from UCLA, where he earned a B.A. in Linguistics, graduating summa cum laude. He subsequently earned his M.A. from Stanford University, where he also was a doctoral candidate and taught in the Linguistics Department, before returning to New Mexico and earning his J.D. from UNM School of Law. Doug was held in the highest regard among his colleagues in the legal profession, having earlier this year been named chair of the copyright section of the state bar. He will also be missed by his many friends in the world of art and theater, and will be remembered for his fund-raising work on behalf of AIDS research.")

Doug's autopsy was conducted on Friday morning, and his house was professionally cleaned later that day. The mortuary transported him in the afternoon, while Bernadette and Pete stood with Greg in his front yard, and two young boys rode past on their bikes. Pete said he needed to get into Doug's study to see if there were any client files. The three walked in and, while Greg and Pete were in the study picking up files from the floor, Bernadette noticed that the *Statue of David* replica was gone from the entryway and that the living room walls now revealed bright blank squares in the fading paint where Doug's abstract lithographs once hung. A cardboard box was on the floor next to a bookshelf. She walked over and looked in. On top were *Further Tales of the City* and two anthologies of gay erotica.

Doug was cremated on Saturday morning. By then, his parents were in his house with Greg. Gone were the AIDS prevention posters from the landing outside his bedroom. They were in the garage with the *Statue of David*, the art, and three cardboard boxes of books and videos. (A couple of months later, when Melissa, her pregnant daughter, and her daughter's fiancé moved in, Mr. Mondragon would drive to Albuquerque in his truck and take these things to the dump, but not before removing the art and posters from their frames, which Melissa would later use for hanging collages of crayon stick figures and green, polka-dotted houses drawn by a grandson named Douglas.)

On Sunday morning, Doug's cremains were poured into a temporary urn and placed upon an altar in the chapel. At 12:45, an organist started playing melodies that no one at first recognized, ending with "Morning Has Broken." The memorial service began promptly at 1:00.

A pastor hired by the mortuary uttered an opening prayer, read passages from the Old and New Testaments, and then spoke to the crowded room. Then Pete stood and gave a short eulogy. He took special care to look at Doug's friends as he spoke, the casual lovers whom Pete had never before seen, most of whom he probably would never see again. Nine rows of friends turned out for Doug, many met on lonely nights in smoky bars, mostly young, save one man in the sixth row who appeared to be around Doug's age. Lawyers too busy to sit, or maybe too afraid, lined the back wall. Some thought they knew why this had happened; others would wonder for the rest of their lives, though their wondering would decrease in frequency over the years. When Pete finished he took his seat next to Bernadette, who was too angry to cry. Doug's aunts were angry, too. They couldn't believe Rose would do it this way, and they would say rosaries and buy mass cards for Doug for the rest of their lives.

By two o'clock, the Mondragons had put a dispersing vessel containing Doug's cremains into their car. They had decided to scatter his ashes into the Rio Grande that afternoon, not far from his house. The river runs through the Mesilla Valley past Las Cruces just a couple hundred miles south of here, they reminded each other, and Doug would be home soon. They stood at the river's edge in silence. Melissa was still sobbing, while Greg stood strong between his parents, his arms across their shoulders. Rose Mondragon's face was red again, and this time her eyes filled as she took a handful of her firstborn's ashes and dropped them into the muddy water. Doug's father whispered something to the box that only he would hear, and then released the rest of his son to the river in a baptism of bone and ash. They drove the four hours back to Las Cruces in silence.

Doug's cremains were split by the current into two distinct, whirling masses within just fifty feet of where they entered the river. One part eventually ran into shallow water and washed up into some salt cedar on the dry, western bank about ten miles south of Albuquerque. Upstream and near the point where they split, the other eddy of floating white particles crossed over a log, and was diverted through an irrigation pipe into the *acequia madre* that runs parallel to the river. From there, the ash and bone traveled through a smaller drain into a North Valley *sangría*, where part was drawn into someone's flower bed by a pump and hose contraption, and where the remainder settled just a day later into the mud of the now waterless ditch.

Billy and the Butte

A T THREE O'CLOCK in the morning the subtle groan of a slowly opening trailer door sounds like a rowboat rubbing against the wharf at the water's edge, sixty yards away. Both are old wood now, the door a weathered, cracking cedar and the boat, fifty-year-old longleaf pine. Though it is hard to discern in the dark, both still show streaks of faded green, traces of younger selves. The door, salvaged from a construction site near El Paso, painted and hung more than three decades ago, now creaks on twisted hinges. And the boat, having traveled in the summer of 1973 from North Carolina to New Mexico, roped to the top of a white Ford pickup truck, still pleads for water, even though its right side is worn to a shine from thirty-five summers of bobbing and rubbing against the wharf on the shore of Elephant Butte Lake. The sounds of old wood—a trailer door, a rowboat. At three in the morning it is hard to tell the difference. But Billy Larson knows. He hung the door, he drove the white pickup.

The blanket is bluish gray, not unlike the water to which it will soon be surrendered, the vast reservoir that swallowed the Rio Grande whole. It is all cotton, loose weave, with the tag still on. Billy purchased it at Wal-Mart in Truth or Consequences in late May, when summer's dry heat is carried into the Mesilla Valley on the shoulders of spring winds, when demand for blankets is measured by limited colors laid on shelves nearly bare. Seven years ago he had used a white blanket, which ended up looking like some muskellunge, belly-up, until it finally gathered enough water to sink to the bottom. Elephant Butte has no muskies, just catfish, stripers, and crappie, largemouth bass in late summer.

From the inside, the blanket is suffocating blackness, with small cotton piles that tickle her nose and cheeks and brush over her eyelids as she struggles to open them against the yarn pressing upon her lashes. At her feet she sees his silhouette, tall and wiry and bent, and feels his bony fingers around her ankles. The itching and smell of the cotton make her want to sneeze, but she knows she must not, lest the weathered man who carries her stiffen at the sound of life within this shroud. She is fully awake now, the throbbing in her swollen head muffled by the cotton. The blanket keeps her warm in the cool night air of this September. It protects the back of her head, covered in long, wavy black hair, and makes for muted thuds against the steps off the trailer porch. *Uno, dos, tres, cuatro, cinco.* And then the hard, uneven ground rises to meet her rear. Her ankles are bound by the blanket, but the knot above her head seems loose. Her hands, believed to be dead, lie free at her sides. She smells the whiskey on his labored, uneven breath.

From the outside, the blanket is a cocoon, wrapped around itself, twisted and tied at each end in old nautical rope from the shed behind Billy's trailer. He holds her bony ankles in his arthritic hands, and winces at the pain in his back as he hunches over and walks slowly backward down the steps off the wooden porch. One, two, three, four, five. And then the hard, uneven ground rises to meet his leather boots. He stops, lowering the blanket to a silent release, climbs the steps, and carefully shuts the trailer door. It groans like the waiting rowboat, listing slowly in the still night, rubbing the wharf to which it is tied. But the neighboring trailers remain dark, no window creaks open, no one presses an ear to the screen, tries to hear.

The sixty yards to the water's edge are stony and rough. Billy moves slowly, stopping intermittently to catch his breath, look over his shoulder, and check the path behind him. The weight of this backward walk begins to bear down upon him, a glaring backlight cast upon his years. He knows every inch of her flesh. Her ankles feel like sharp stone in his hands, he can almost see her round rump and stout shoulders bouncing off the clumps of sagebrush and around the rocks to the dusty ground. The weight of a backward walk. But he knows this path, knows this walk. Each September for the past seven years, when all the thousands of thirsty New Mexicans have packed their coolers and tents, their boats and water skis and RVs, and have returned to their dry cities and towns, to Albuquerque and Socorro and beyond, he has taken this backward, slow, dark walk.

The young women arrive in Truth or Consequences each May, a few days before Memorial Day. They roam dark edges of parking lots and sit at red, plastic-covered bar stools in the lounges along Main Street, where they pull at loose Scotch tape that sticks to their tight yellow and chartreuse pants, and where Travis Tritt and Pat Boone can be heard simultaneously blasting from jukeboxes in a language they do not understand. They pose on benches along Broadway and twist ribbons and paper flowers into their hair and paint their nails red, and they linger behind yuccas that blend into the landscape at McDonald's. By the beginning of the weekend, when the town is filled to overflowing with a strange concoction of drunk college students from Las Cruces, retired fishermen and their wives who travel the last of their tired lives in RVs, and families hauling speedboats and jet skis from Albuquerque, the young women are mostly twisted about on rumpled sheets in the cramped rooms of cheap motels that dot the road to Elephant Butte, their colorful pants and white ruffled blouses flung over some windowsill, or hanging off some straight-backed chair under which they have placed their sparkling, sequined sandals. Some are in the smoky cabs at the truck stop north of town, others in lower bunks at the RV park. Carmen Rodriguez Bustillos, of Villa Ahumada, eighty miles south of Ciudad Juárez, is subconsciously moving to the rhythm of the lapping waters of Elephant Butte she hears outside the window, wondering if she can send money home before the end of summer, and twitching at the scratchy fiber of the shag carpet as it rubs beneath her bare knees in Billy Larson's trailer.

By the first week of June he has found her four times, driven her to the trailer and dropped her off two hours later in front of the Texaco station in Truth or Consequences, money in hand. She finds him no more disgusting than any of the rest. He is fairly clean, save the layers of grease under his fingernails and the subtle smells of whiskey and smoke that seem to permanently emanate from deep within his stomach, no matter the half-empty bottle of Listerine mouthwash that sits above the bathroom sink. His medicine chest contains a blue toothbrush, a tube of Colgate toothpaste, a razor, a black comb, and three miscellaneous pill bottles. He seems to have only one towel, but she lacks the nerve to open the metal cabinet that stands across from the toilet, for fear the turning handles might be heard from the bedroom. By the first week of June, all she knows about him, other than the obvious, is that he has a television in the living room across from a sofa and chair, he fries hamburger in the greasy iron skillet that sits on the stove, and in the bedroom he has a closet whose door is kept closed. There is a dilapidated wooden shed behind the trailer, with tools stacked on a workbench near its door. She does not care to know more. If she did, she would know that he has a Purple Heart in a plastic box under the telephone book in his nightstand, a grown daughter he never knew in Bien Hoa and, in his wallet, a black-and-white photograph of him and his father sitting in the rowboat in the summer of 1952, when he was only five years old. If she cared, she would know that the photo captures the last time he ever laid eyes on his mother.

By the middle of June, after trying three other girls, he has chosen her. He finds her no less disgusting than any of the rest. She is short and round, with long black hair and brown eyes that sharply contrast with her pale, doughy skin. She carries a straw satchel that contains a single key with the words No Duplicate, a tissue folded over a rosary with pink beads, a red lipstick, a black comb, and a leather coin purse.

He suspects she carries her cash in a separate location, perhaps in her clothing somewhere, but he lacks the nerve to open the coin purse, for fear the snap of the clasp might be heard from the bathroom. By the middle of June, all he knows about her, other than the obvious, is that she has no fear of him, this is her first season here, and her name is Carmen. She is perhaps sixteen years old, and will likely be missed by no one. He does not care to know more. If he did, he would know that she is actually nineteen, her little son lives with her father, her three sisters, and her aunt in a twelve-by-eight-foot shanty made of scrap mesquite and rusty, corrugated tin, and she was crowned queen of the *Fiestas patronales de Santa María Magdalena* when she was only seven years old. If he cared, he would know that her mother, part Apache, died alone in the desert the next day.

The last Thursday of June began like the previous nights. Billy cruised up and down Broadway and then Main Street, until he spotted Carmen walking out of Boater's Lounge, honked the horn, and then parked around the corner with the engine on until she climbed in. It was uneventful, from the twenty-minute drive to the trailer, to the bolting of its creaky door behind them, to the walk across the living room and into the bedroom. She carefully hung her clothes over the corner chair and placed her sandals underneath, while Billy brushed his teeth in the bathroom. She did not notice the clank of the metal cabinet's turning handles, but she felt a flood of adrenaline when Billy returned to the bedroom, completely dressed and carrying a worn leather gag that went over her mouth so tight and so fast that she did not even have time to inhale. When the closet door opened, revealing not shirts or shoes or jackets but, instead, a small room containing at its center a suspended cage shaped like a spiderweb, surrounded by whips and collars and clamps and cuffs and god-knows-what hanging from the walls, she felt her body go stiff and her head go light. It would be one of the last times that summer those parts of her would feel connected.

By early July she had given up trying to find ways to escape, or to get someone's attention. She could hardly hear her own muffled cries.

And of those with whom she had crossed that dry riverbed, who would miss a girl named Carmen? Her father and sisters and aunt in Villa Ahumada, picturing her mopping floors or washing dishes, would not even think to miss her until autumn. She could imagine her son sleeping peacefully, curled between the protective arms of her *tía*, his head resting on her ample breast, and then laughing in the mornings at the antics of her youngest sister. By August, she had stopped thinking even of him. Instead, she recited rosaries in her head and the words to every song she ever knew, though she was no longer prayerful, and the melodies had escaped her. But the rhythm of the words kept her from feeling the totality of the blistering whippings, the contortions of her bones, the cruel invasions. She did not even notice that it had all stopped by September.

The men at Henry's Marine noticed nothing different about Billy Larson that summer. There was nothing different to notice. Billy would show up at the service bay by eight o'clock every morning, and while he preferred Mercury outboards, he could handle a Cobra stern drive easily, pick it up from the marina, change the gear oil, grease the gimbals, drain the block, manifold, and hoses, and install a new water pump, all by noon. He would come back after lunch and do it again, though he would talk less and move slower. If they had paid more attention they would have noticed that by July, his lunches lasted longer and that by August, his breath carried the slight scent of liquor first thing in the mornings. If they had paid more attention they would have noticed that by September, he had called in four times over his allowable number of sick days. But the men at Henry's Marine were not a curious group. In all the years Billy had worked there, no one had ever asked him about the Purple Heart license plate on his truck, or where he got his southern accent. No one knew his mother had been beaten to death when he was five years old, or that he carried that old picture of him and his father in his wallet.

He took a long road back to the trailer that September evening. He pulled out of Henry's Marine just after five o'clock and headed north paralleling the Butte, the sun low on the water and splashing pink across the towering dam. He ignored the turnoff to the trailer park and kept going north, passing Long Point and Three Sisters before turning around on the gravel ramp above South Monticello Point. By the time he passed Three Sisters again, he had decided on tonight. It was not so much a decision as instinct, maybe habit. As he approached his turnoff, he pulled over, cast his tired eyes through binoculars across the lake, adjusted his focus on the adobe foundations of old Fort McRae emerging from the receding waters just under the bluffs of Champagne Hills, and thought not of the slaughter of Apaches as they traveled the Jornada del Muerto, but for the first time of how low the water level had become.

He drank for hours that night, rambling wildly about his mother and father, and showed her the tattered picture from the wallet and the Purple Heart from the nightstand.

"She hollers for us to smile, takes the goddamn picture, then walks up the fucking hill and we don't see her again until they find her dead whore body in the woods behind the motel!" he screams.

He rips off his shirt and shows her the ragged scar running down the deep indentation in his left shoulder, nearly to his elbow, where a sergeant's strong bicep once was. He points to a small scar on his right temple, to an old gash across his chest.

"I have a fucking plate in my arm! I make it through Tet without a scratch. And then, right before I'm supposed to get choppered out to R-and-R, I get shot by one of my own guys—some fucking grunt on the edge of the delta who's not paying attention. I'm lying there and half my fucking arm is hanging off a tree limb, I can't see shit for the blood, and all this dumb fuck can say is that he's sorry and he'll make it up to me someday!"

She understood not a word, only that he spoke. He talked about the other women, how they looked and what they wore, and even how they smelled.

Then he said, "You're a real beaut, you know? Beaut? Butte? Get it?"

He laughed and spit, but she did not get it. That was when he unchained her and threw her head against the wall. She did not know about the sofa cushion over her face, or the bluish gray blanket he had stashed in the metal cabinet in the bathroom.

At four o'clock in the morning the slapping of water, one tired hand at a time, sounds like the torn and weathered American flag whipping about in the wind that has suddenly arisen over the open lake. All colors are faded now. The tired hands are pale and reddish, the lips faintly blue, as she emerges from the blanket and swims through a second baptism toward the safety of Fort McRae. And the flag has been waving above the rowboat since a September past when towers in the sky, like a girl named Carmen, went missing. The sounds of tired hands upon the water, a flag in the wind. At four in the morning it is hard to tell the difference. But Carmen Rodriguez Bustillos knows. The hands are hers, the flags are everywhere.

My Summer Home

IT IS WITH much sadness I write on the occasion of the loss of my summer home. I won't keep you in suspense. It was consumed by a raging fire six months ago. I lost nearly everything, but managed to grab my most treasured possessions as I raced through the dark in a choking smoke—a birch wagon my grandmother gave me in 1961, in it my dissertation, a ragged photograph of me on some water's edge when I was six, a few miscellaneous household items wrapped in some seasonal articles of clothing, an old throw pillow, its purple cover faded and held fast with three rusted safety pins.

I could have been more practical and grabbed the duct tape, maybe some garbage bags, my medications. Instead, in the middle of my panic, I was pitched into a salty sea of sentiment and went for the photo, the pillow. Adrenaline is a most interesting substance. Think of the accident victim whose life flashes before his proverbial eyes as he lies dying alone in the night on some unforgiving, icy patch of asphalt, his motorcycle still roaring as though it might somehow rise up, disentangle itself from the bent spruce, and drive him home. He thinks not of the note left on the kitchen counter by his cheating wife, or of the anger he tried to wash away at Bobby's Tavern three miles back. Instead, as blood drains from his left ear and begins to freeze in gelatinous pools beneath his head, his heart hums along with his grandmother's favorite song ("You are my sunshine, my only sunshine...," her low voice would whisper in his ear as she wrapped the purple afghan around him). He is warm with hot chocolate, a fire casts itself across her living room walls; he is three years old and spending the night. Or imagine the young woman upon learning of her husband's death in a convenience store robbery committed at eight that morning, as he stopped for his usual cup of coffee. She does not scream, she does not weep. Instead, she smiles and says over and over again to the police chaplain, "He's going to take me out to dinner and a movie tonight; it's my birthday." Just then a flower delivery van pulls up to the curb, carrying the bouquet of red roses and blue Dutch irises he had ordered the day before. "It's my birthday."

I digress.

What I miss most are the cottonwoods that surrounded my home and stood like sentries standing guard in the night over me. Their green canopies held nests of great horned owls, red-tailed hawks; their sturdy trunks bore the teeth marks of beavers that came up from the river's bank to feed at dawn. Oh, this river, it runs like lifeblood through my heart. I miss its slow meandering through the bosque, the bats skimming its surface at dusk. My neighbors and I would often sit with cocktails at the water's edge. When darkness fell, one of the men would light a fire, grill some catfish he had caught earlier in the day. Rock squirrels bounced through my front yard; I even saw a bobcat on a late August afternoon. I would wake to the cries of coyotes howling at night, then fall back asleep to the boundless sounds of life along the Rio Grande, the croaking of a bullfrog, the rustling of leaves followed by a subtle splash as a hungry muskrat took to the muddy water.

My neighbor was falsely charged with setting the fire. Phil was quiet—a skinny, bearded Vietnam vet who preferred living alone, reading his Bible, spreading seed for the quail, and sketching the ring-necked pheasants in, of all things, pencil. But he lost everything, too. And he hadn't hurt a soul since 1969, when he was just a kid in a mountain near the DMZ. No, Phil did not set the fire. I saw two teenage boys at the water's edge that afternoon. They didn't belong there. They arrived on shiny, expensive bicycles, wore soccer shorts, colorful jerseys, sunglasses like the kind you see on movie stars in the magazine rack at Walgreens. One of them had a stash of firecrackers, which they took turns lighting and tossing into the river. Only they didn't all land in the water. That night, as my neighbors and I gathered in the parking lot of the Sonic with our meager possessions, our neighborhood burning directly to the west, the police honed in on Phil, who was by then alternately chain-smoking and fiddling with his lighter. "River rat been drinking tonight? Have a few cigarettes, maybe left one of them burning?" The questions never stopped, and an old anger rose up in Phil. Like I said, he hadn't hurt anyone since 1969. But then he just erupted from somewhere deep inside and hit the older cop in the face. It took three other cops to wrestle him down, cuff him, and toss him into the squad car. With the shock of the fire and evacuation, I was unable to tell the police about the two boys on the bicycles. Instead, I just whispered over and over, "It wasn't Phil; it wasn't Phil." I might have said more, had anyone bothered to ask.

My summer home was nestled in a small clearing among a thicket of salt cedar and surrounded by cottonwoods on three sides. A stand of Russian olive trees protected it from the east; there was a wonderful view of the river. And I walked nearly every morning. In a matter of minutes I could be on the bike path behind the zoo, see the elephants feeding in the back of their pen (at night I could hear the roar of the lions, then would dream I was in Africa). Just north of the zoo was Tingley Beach. I would stop and rest on one of its wrought-iron benches, watch the old men fish, the children chase the geese. In the fall of 1962, my grandmother and I would take lazy walks along that old lagoon. When I would tire, she would haul me around in the birch wagon. One October day she brought her Brownie camera and asked an old man to take our picture. At the last second, just when the man said, "Say cheese," I felt her hand rest upon my shoulder. As we ate our lunch, a flock of sandhill cranes flew over in a V-formation, and I thought they sounded like a pack of barking dogs. "They're following the Rio Grande to their winter home," my grandmother said. "If you look up and save a place in the sky, they'll return again in spring. No matter which way they're flying, they're always headed for home." She gave me that picture a week later. It's the one I saved from the fire, though someone tore it in half when I was seven, threw away the part that showed my grandmother, and shoved the remaining half into the pocket of my blue corduroy jacket. I look at that picture every day. I'm standing at the edge of the lagoon, and though I appear to be alone, there remains a strong hand upon my shoulder; I know who was at my side. Above me is an abundant sky. I would think of that day twice each year, as I walked the clear ditch east of my summer home, the sandhill cranes soaring overhead. And twice each year I would save that same place in the sky, between springtime and October.

I cannot complain.

Now I walk from my cozy downtown spot to the office in a matter of minutes. And passersby bestow upon me all the supplies I require— blank pads of paper, pens (lots of pens), the occasional notebook which I can fill on a good morning. A man who walks by each day recently left some poster board and blue magic markers. "Someday I would like to see what you are writing," he said. Well, if he must know, I'm re-working my dissertation. But I keep getting stuck around the various factors that go into a decision to seal a mine after a collapse. My advisor made various suggestions thirty years ago, and I've been working on it ever since. When it was first suggested I make changes, I admit I protested. In fact, for three months I did little but sit cross-legged on the speckled linoleum floor outside the department chair's office. When that failed to change my advisor's mind (and after the university police had escorted me off campus for the fourth time), I set about to rewrite the dissertation from scratch. But I would get only so far, when life would interrupt. The third marriage was an unmitigated disaster. Did I ever mention Frieda, my longhaired calico? She was rather nasty to all but me, and shed like a molting mallard in spring. But she generally perched on just one chair, an antique oak rocker with a throw pillow on it. Well, Frieda died in the fall of 1993, leaving her furry mess all over that chair and pillow. My husband drank too much that Thanksgiving, and threatened to burn down the house if I didn't get rid of the fur. So I cut some purple chenille from the back of the sofa, where no one could see, and re-upholstered the chair and pillow, leaving Frieda's fur hidden safe below. He left me anyway. I don't know what happened to that chair, but I kept the pillow. In fact, in 1995 I deliberately slit open the back and fastened it with three safety pins, so I could finger the downy softness of Frieda's fur whenever I felt the need. I swear I can still smell her.

Forgive me.

I built my summer home over two years ago. The city had become too much, the heat rising from the downtown pavement at noon so oppressive that I had taken to working on my dissertation at a corner table in the cool of Java Joe's, a small coffee shop down the alley and around the corner from where I lived. I wouldn't return home until an evening breeze could air it out. To pass time, I began perusing the *Alibi*, a free weekly paper in the stand on the sidewalk outside the coffee shop. Before long, I would just skip to the personals—Women Seeking Men, Men Seeking Women, Alternatives. And then there was the "I Saw You" section, an intriguing array of hope splattered in black ink upon the last page of the personals.

"You—tall, blonde, wearing blue skirt, looked my way last Friday at Sauce. Me—athletic, white T-shirt and jeans at next table; let's talk."

"You—Presbyterian Hospital elevator late morning of June 4, our eyes met. Me—red shorts, still out of breath from my run. Lunch or dinner?"

The following week one suddenly stood out. "You—faded denim skirt, mismatched sneakers, very tan, corner table at Java Joe's, would love to meet." I glanced quickly at my shoes. Could this be?

The following week, "You—long silver hair, UNM sweatshirt with sleeves rolled up, writing madly at Java Joe's."

"You—purple ski hat, orange silk scarf…"

I began testing this for other locations I would frequent, the concrete benches next to the fountain at Civic Plaza ("You—writing letters in Civic Plaza…"), the park near Bank of America ("You—crossing Wells Park on Friday, ran down 6th and slipped behind bank before I could catch up…"), the post office ("You—filling cup from water fountain at main post office…"). What flattery! I could barely sleep. I even took the bus up Central one day to peer through the window of the *Alibi* office and see if I could discover the identity of my mysterious suitor. But all I saw was my own reflection in the glass. I decided to try a more refined setting, in the hopes of getting an invitation to meet. Now, some would say I have fine dining taste. This is surely overstated, but I have been known to enjoy Café Benoit's grilled salmon with slivered almonds atop the arugula salad. I only lack a sip of latte to accompany the occasional bite of crème caramel or lemon tart for dessert.

It worked.

"You—eating alone, Café Benoit, midnight. Me—passerby in search of dining companion with discriminating tastes. Meet next Saturday night, table for two at last window."

I showered, did my hair, even found an old blouse with a lovely floral print that still flattered my figure, and set out for Café Benoit promptly at eight the next Saturday evening. I was just about to walk around the corner to the front of the building, when some unfortunate tiff arose between the chef and headwaiter, who were smoking outside the back door. Before I could get by them, the chef yelled at me, "I told you to stay away from the fucking dumpster!" I was stunned. This sent me rushing into the streets in search of any welcoming place, maybe another inviting café where a handsome stranger might be seated alone at a small table by a back window, nervously fingering a rose corsage, gazing at a candle that still flickered in the waning light. I hurried through the streets of downtown, past young couples in line to get into clubs, patios filled with weekend diners. Their lips were moving, some leaned forward in their chairs nodding their heads intently at their companions across from them, others, their necks reared back and mouths agape in laughter. I saw wine glasses clinking in toasts, smiles all around. But all I could hear was the clatter of forks, fine china cups colliding with matching saucers, a cacophonous conversation of utensils upon plates. I peered through every restaurant window. There was no handsome stranger. I ended up back at Java Joe's just before closing, exhausted, a blister forming on my left heel.

The following week's *Alibi* read, "You—staring into your half-full coffee mug, blue eyes gone gray. Me—you."

I started my summer home in the bosque the following week, and put my dissertation on hold until fall.

All behind me now.

In the months since the fire, I have been scraping and saving to rebuild. I have a pile of branches hidden among the salt cedar, and I bought some duct tape and garbage bags at the Walgreens across from Old Town. I'll have to site my summer home a bit south this time, where the cottonwoods still grow. But there is a rusted jetty jack between the levee trail and my new lot, which should help keep out undesirables, like boys on shiny bikes, or phantom suitors. From now on, only the real thing for me. Yes, I shall return to the quiet of my river, let its coursing waters quench my heart's thirst, baptize my blood. I shall take long naps under the abundant sky, let it warm me like a grandmother's afghan. I saw Phil recently, and he also expressed a desire to rebuild near the river. Hopefully, the other neighbors will return as well. And my dissertation, though still in need of some polishing, is clearly in its final stages. I shall prepare its defense soon. For now, though, I must cut this short. It is Wednesday night, and the housekeepers come tomorrow. I must gather my things and move to the bus shelter across from the parking garage, as the truck picks up at the first light of dawn.

The Mayordomo's Son

I F NOT FOR the rusted headgate, padlocked and chained, that early April night would not have been the only night of love you ever made. For a lifetime you would have conjured the rich smell of fresh earth on your skin, felt new blades of grass soft beneath you, small miracles bursting through a parched ground. You would have seen the horizon's dark blue slip to black as you gazed just beyond his undulant shoulders; you would have seen the Seven Sisters appear in the western sky. The cadence of his sharp, shallow breathing would have played in pulsing counterpoint to the steady breeze that moved through the willows, as his short and strong body moved quietly into yours. The mayordomo's son. You would have forever seen those almond-shaped eyes, set deep below thick black hair. If not for the rusted headgate, padlocked and chained, you would have recalled that April night's sweetness for all your days, and Ramón Castillo would have wrapped your years in kindness as he did your young flesh in his gentleness.

Instead, you remembered the driving beat of your father's old leather boots, growing more purposeful with each nearing step. You could almost see the dust kick up behind each pounding heel; you could imagine each pointed toe piercing the ground. Your breathing stopped with the groan of the pine door to the toolshed behind which you lay, and you heard him mumble something about the pipe cutter. As your skin grew cold with fear, he appeared like a specter from around the side of the toolshed, the pipe cutter slung over his shoulder and reflecting on and off under the full moon like the dying lamp flickering through your distant kitchen window. He passed just ten feet from where you and Ramón Castillo lay frozen to the spring earth, his silhouette casting a strangely large shadow upon the shed wall, the pine door swinging to and fro and crying like a trapped wolf in the growing wind.

The snapping of the padlock and freeing of the chain rang sharp against the night, followed by the slow grinding of the cast-iron handwheel. As the stubborn stem slowly gave way and the headgate cover creaked open, you could almost see the flakes of rust falling through your father's hands, the muscles of his sweaty forearms contracting, his slate-blue eyes set in steely determination. Then, in a glistening flash that cast him in a garish backlight, the rushing water surged through the gate, ran down the ditch, and poured into his thirsty fields. He stood there for half an hour, shoulders bent with sorrow, or maybe with just the times and, even then, with Ramón Castillo motionless at your side, you felt your father's weariness penetrate deep below your own skin, almost touching bone—the whole weariness of 1929 when everything seemed to be breaking—the farms and banks, the cycles of rain, Hoover's promises, the headgate to your father's piece of the ditch.

If the closing of a padlock could be measured in ticks of time, as with a metronome, then it could be said the first beat happened just a year earlier when the wire fence to your father's sheep pen tore loose from its post, and two sheep were seen drinking at the ditch's edge, a violation of *Acequia de Corrales* rules that prohibited the grazing of livestock along the banks. Then, just a few days later, one of your father's laborers was caught washing his clothes in the common ditch and discarding some old rags into the clear waters. Pablo Castillo had been elected mayordomo for the fourth time the previous January, along with three new commissioners, and had just started the season's water distribution. In prosperous times the fines would have been affordable, and Pablo

Castillo and his sons even helped repair the broken fence the following Sunday, but the infractions became a permanent part of the mayordomo's journal, and your father's inability to pay all at once left a scarlet delinquency showing in the treasurer's ledger. Then, a month later, the delinquency was tripled when your father, having taken suddenly ill, failed to tend the sluice to his laterals one afternoon, and his ditches overflowed in a virtual bloodletting that broke through earthen berms and flooded the adjacent road and an uncultivated field with waters too precious to waste. If the closing of a padlock could be measured in ticks of a metronome, or if a chain could be seen tightening in upon itself one steel link at a time, then your father could have felt the early onset of thirst that year, the dry scratchiness one feels in the back of the throat just before the glass goes empty.

Instead, he begged and borrowed all through fall and winter, selling his horses and mortgaging half of the next year's crop, and managed to pay down nearly two-thirds of his delinquency by late January, when he cast his forty votes for the reelection of Pablo Castillo. And then, just before the annual March ditch cleaning, when every farmer raked and shoveled and sweat in exact proportion to the amount of his own ditch frontage, when weeds were scraped and berms rebuilt, when broken headgates and earthen dams were repaired, the bank failed and his line of credit went dry as the valley. He could no longer pay for the four laborers he was to provide; the cart and scraper he was to supply sat dusty and idle behind the stall that once held the two horses he had hoped to redeem.

Even as you held your breath that early April night and watched the forbidden waters flood your father's fields, not daring to move and hoping against hope he would take some mysterious, inexplicable turn, grow smaller along some illogical path back to the house, even as you awaited that terrible, inevitable discovery, even then you felt the sting of your father's shame like a weighted strap across your naked back, the mayordomo's son a reluctant witness. You thought not of Ramón Castillo's warmth, still wet upon your thigh, but of seasons when rain was plentiful and promises were easier kept, times when water need not be stolen, when it came from the sky's generosity and flew off snowcapped mountains, fed the Rio Grande, filled the *Acequia de Corrales*, and then baptized your father's forty acres.

During the annual water rotations your father's fields would flow three days each month, April through October. You watched that part of the earth turn green with corn and peppers and squash that went each autumn down a rutted road in a wagon roped to the back of your father's old Model T, and east across the narrow bridge to Albuquerque's market. The rest went pickled and canned to your mother's cold cellar, and then one glass jar at a time up the narrow stairs to your kitchen, aglow in a steady light, all winter long. It fed you and your six sisters, and each May it helped feed all your neighbors at the *Fiesta de San Ysidro Labrador,* when your mother and all the other mothers heaped mounds of fresh irises, red roses, and lilac cuttings on the altar, and when your father and all the other fathers carried the wooden, carved *santo* to a hill above the fields to watch over the crops until harvest. (Once, your father and Pablo Castillo sat on a Sunday morning under a willow tree behind a toolshed and agreed that Ramón Castillo could take you to the fiesta dance, but only if he brought you home by ten o'clock. They did not know you and he had already met four times behind Miller's Mercantile, had taken afternoon walks along the Rio Grande, and had dangled your legs over its low banks, four bare feet touching just below the surface of its shallow, muddy waters.)

But all that was before the drought, before Hoover. "Spend," he had said. And your father and the rest of the country spent, until there was nothing left and they were all spent themselves. "The poorhouse is vanishing from among us," he promised. And your father and all the others believed, until they opened their eyes one day and found themselves surrounded by the peeling and cracked walls of the poor houses they once called home. "The fundamental business of the country... is on a sound and prosperous basis," he lied. And by then it was just too late. Too late for your father, for Pablo Castillo, for everyone. The headgate rusted from lack of grease, its wood went rotten. The concrete crumbled and the frame fell loose. That March your father, who refused to let his fields go fallow, could no longer pay for workers to clear his piece of the ditch, and the mayordomo had no choice but to padlock and chain his headgate, and to let the waters flow past the newly sown ground.

If not for the rusted headgate, padlocked and chained, that April night would have played in your mind like a perfectly tuned cello, danced before your eyes in a perfectly choreographed ballet. Instead, your heart pounded nearly through your bare breast as your father's footsteps again drew close. And then he stopped. You turned away in muted resignation and watched the night play out in a cast of flailing shadows, and in ghostly reflections of the pipe cutter projected like a moving picture against the toolshed wall. Your father's words and Ramón's pleadings burst through the dark and combined in a clashing, cacophonous symphony, an orchestra pitted against itself. And Ramón Castillo's gentleness was suddenly drowned in the blood that gushed from his face and ran down his chest, and poured in streams from the gashes on his back as he ran naked into that night. And then that word, not spoken before and never spoken again, the kind of word used by people like your father (but never him), people who came from places like western Pennsylvania, or maybe Ohio, that kind of word fabricated for people different from your own, came flying out of his mouth in a burst of spit from somewhere far behind his clenched teeth and ricocheted like a bullet against the night. "Spic!" And the mayordomo's son grew smaller in the distance, until he was forever gone.

You never remembered the walk back, only the flickering light through the kitchen window, as though the farmhouse was somehow approaching you, as though you somehow remained forever fixed to that spot of earth behind the toolshed. You never recalled the feel of Ramón Castillo's last touch upon your skin, a cold hand on your thigh, as he rose from the ground upon which you lay.

That summer's silence was broken just once when your father, polishing his spectacles with the tattered lace napkin, and looking up from his plate of beans and potatoes to some patch of peeling, cracked plaster on the wall just beyond your shoulder, quietly said, "You shall be sent to the Colorado State Normal School in August, and your mother shall take to her room with one of her spells." And to your six sisters, the kind of question to which no answer is possible, "Do you understand?"

––––––––––

If not for the rusted headgate, padlocked and chained, the child's name would have been Katherine. But your parents called her Mary Elizabeth. By the time you returned to the farmhouse (just a house now, since the conservancy district tore through the valley and stole all the ditches, and ran your father and Pablo Castillo and everyone else from their fields), she was three years old. If not for the rusted headgate, padlocked and chained, twenty years later you, dressed in an emerald velvet gown with matching hat and satin gloves, would have watched her marry from your seat in the first row of pews at San Ysidro Church. Her almond-shaped eyes would have sparkled at you from behind a white veil as she strode by, short and strong, her hair cascading in thick black waves over her shoulders and down her back. Instead, you stood smiling by her side at the altar wearing the same peach cotton dress as your six lanky sisters beside you. If not for the rusted headgate, padlocked and chained, you would have sat all in black thirty-nine years later in that same pew, the lace veil moving softly across your lined face, your silver hair pinned beneath and falling in tired wisps along the back of your neck, your head bent in sorrow as some young priest spoke kind, unknowing words of her. Instead, you sat with your two remaining sisters in the third row, just behind Mary Elizabeth's husband, four sons, and all their wives and children.

You nearly gave yourself away only three times. Once, at a dinner given in your honor for having taught at Los Ranchitos Elementary School for forty years, you were heard to say of Mary Elizabeth's sons, "No one will ever know what those boys mean to me." Then, over a decade later, you were told Mary Elizabeth had Hodgkin's disease. The sharp intake of breath, along with the simultaneous raising of your hand to your mouth, was well within the realm of predictable reactions. But then you whispered, to no one in particular and with your hand still over your mouth, as though to keep the words from spilling out, tumbling over your lips, and falling to the floor in some clattering, rolling heap, "That's what Ramón Castillo died of." And then just last week you, no longer able to bear the weight of your ninety-four years, closed your eyes, made the sign of the cross and died on, of all days, Mother's Day.

No one knew your last thoughts were of a rusted headgate, padlocked and chained—not Mary Elizabeth's sons, not your nieces and nephews who stood by your hospital bed and witnessed what seemed, from all appearances (indeed, what was written in your obituary), a peaceful death. But if not for that rusted headgate, padlocked and chained, her name would have been Katherine. She would have been born a half mile from the Rio Grande in the warm parlor of some small adobe house, luminous with firelight, flames licking at the crackling piñon and casting delicate reflections across the four sturdy walls; she would have been swaddled in a quilt your mother made, then handed to the mayordomo's son. Instead, she was stolen from you in the middle of a bitter December night by three nuns in a stone outbuilding behind a monastery above the Pecos, and secreted to your father's waiting car. If not for the rusted headgate, padlocked and chained, that December night would have been filled with the promise of all the seasons to come, like an *acequia madre* with an abundant spring runoff. Instead, you shivered in the cold, clenched your teeth, and in a quaking, silent shudder, gave birth to the last of your seven sisters.

The Great Lunch Debates of 1960

THEIR VOICES RICOCHET like bullets across the years, all those angry men shouting, "Open the curtains, open the goddamn curtains all the way!" We sat high above and just to Nixon's left at the Civic Auditorium, and the green velvet stage curtains billowed in the noonday October breeze that slipped like a specter through the building's open doors, intermittently blocking the view of the podium. I had no idea what Nixon was saying, only that he and my parents and all those angry men wanted him to be president. If I could have flown, I would have sailed over that sea of people like a trapeze artist, grabbed the draw cord, and swung on it until the curtains were fully open. Instead, I alternately put my hands over my ears and hummed, and picked at the bologna in my teeth, until my father put his index finger to his pursed lips, and my mother whispered through a clenched jaw to get my hands out of my mouth. My older brother Jeff, who was annoyed that my parents had pulled him out of school for this occasion, kept poking me in the side and whispering, "He's an ugly goon; Grandma's right." My mother glared at him, while my father hollered about the curtains.

Having overheard my parents discussing the logistics of seeing the vice president during the lunch hour, I had imagined us sitting in some

elegant parlor appointed with Victorian furniture and crystal chande-
liers, quietly eating our sandwiches while my parents spoke in hushed
tones with Mr. and Mrs. Nixon. Instead, that morning my mother
yelled at us to get out of the kitchen, while she hurriedly slathered
Miracle Whip, margarine, and French's mustard on Wonder bread,
and slapped bologna between the slices. She wrapped the sandwiches
in plastic, whisked raspberry Kool-Aid into a pitcher of tepid water,
poured the swirling mixture into my father's plaid work thermos, and
threw it all in a grocery bag along with a handful of paper napkins and
an open package of Oreos.

My little sister and I shared the thermos cup. We ate quietly in the
backseat of our blue '54 Ford Customline in the parking lot of the
Civic, while my father and Jeff saved our place in the long line. I took
only a few bites of the bologna sandwich, and then wadded it into the
napkin and stuffed it behind the seat.

That night my grandmother came over for supper, and I pulled at her
skirt and excitedly exclaimed, "We saw Nixon, we saw him!" She shot
me an unfamiliar look from across the table, then asked, "And what did
he have to say for himself?"

My father glared at his mother, as I replied, "I don't know. Everybody
was mad. We had bologna sandwiches in the car."

She left when my sister locked herself in the bathroom for the second
time that evening.

A few weeks later my grandmother picked me up to spend the night
at her house in Corrales. "We'll have a picnic tomorrow at Tingley
Beach, and you can feed the ducks in the lagoon," she said loudly, as
my mother muttered something while packing my overnight bag in the
next room. Her strong hands gripped the wheel tight as we sped across
the river and bounced along the winding dirt roads that led to her old
adobe at the edge of the *acequia madre*, the mother ditch that paralleled
the Rio Grande, and fed all its irrigation channels.

That afternoon I played on the banks of the clear ditch until nearly
dark, as my grandmother watched from the kitchen window, her long

silver hair backlit by the oil lamp she kept burning on the pine side-board. We had butternut squash soup and warm rolls, and then spent the evening making Boston brown bread. My grandmother filled a cast-iron kettle halfway with water and set it to boil on the stove, while I buttered the Maryland Club coffee can.

"You're a good helper," she said in her soft voice, ignoring the drops of blackstrap molasses dripping from her counter and pooling into a sticky mess on the floor, along with the buttermilk I had already spilled on the way from the icebox on the back porch. Together we spooned the batter into the coffee can, and covered it with wax paper. My grandmother then covered the can with foil, tied it with string, and placed it carefully on a rack inside the kettle of boiling water.

The covered kettle went into the oven, and in two hours it came out and filled my grandmother's kitchen with a sweet steam that perme-ated the walls and fogged the windows. We played checkers late into the night while the can cooled, and then my grandmother put me in bed and blanketed me against the cold in an afghan, blue to match my eyes, she said.

The next morning we packed a basket with the brown bread, some sliced apples from the tree outside the back door, and a thermos of cold milk. Her faded, green 1948 Dodge rumbled across the bridge to Albu-querque and rattled along North Fourth to downtown, then suddenly turned east.

"Where are we?" I said, as we pulled into the parking lot of a football stadium.

"It's a surprise," she said with a wink.

We waited for an hour on bleachers warmed by the morning sun when, to a joyous roar, came a parade of waving men in polished lim-ousines. The motorcade circled the track twice and then, from a black convertible, emerged John Kennedy. I don't recall what he said, but he was handsome and had a huge smile with lots of teeth, and my grand-mother's eyes filled with tears, the good kind.

On our way out, my grandmother picked up a button with his photo on it and pinned it to my blue corduroy coat. I stared out the car window as we slowly made our way out of the parking lot. Everyone was smiling, just like Kennedy.

By the time we arrived at Tingley, there were only a few old men still fishing. A lone mallard dipped its head below the water, as if performing some baptism of self. As we ate our lunch at the weathered picnic table, a flock of sandhill cranes flew over in an unfamiliar cacophony, not yet roosted in my memory. "They're following the Rio Grande south to their winter home," my grandmother explained. "If you save a place in the sky, they'll return again in springtime."

They're all gone now, first Kennedy and my grandmother, then Nixon (my parents voted for him again in 1968, and I sent a dollar to his campaign because he had a secret plan to get us out of the war). My father rests in the soft earth beneath a twisted cottonwood; my mother's skin turned yellow in her last year, like a watered-down rum and Coke. The corduroy coat grew small, and was passed down to my sister. It finally went threadbare in 1964, but not before the Kennedy pin was lost in the sandy reaches of some playground. The Civic Auditorium, its halls gone silent and empty, was eventually torn down. Jeff graduated high school from there in 1969, the green curtains a ghostly backdrop. My parents gave him the '54 Ford. The spring before he went to Vietnam, he removed the backseat to reupholster it and found my bologna sandwich still wrapped in its paper napkin, the bologna shriveled and dry like leather, the bread hard and dusty. We lost him in 1970, and now bits of his bones have gone to dust somewhere beneath the mud along the Mekong.

I still walk the Corrales clear ditch, never far from my grandmother's old house. My shoulders bow beneath the weight of the years; my pace has slowed. And though my focus has shifted more toward the sand beneath my feet, I still look to the sky twice each year when I hear that familiar cry high above the river. My own grandson was born two springs ago, as the sandhill cranes flew north for home. My wish for him is a life measured by seasons more than my brother ever knew—seasons heralded by the steadfast choirs of cranes, not the angry trumpets of wars—until the last great bird passes south overhead on the winds of some cold, October dusk.

The Night Smarty Reagan
Took the Triple Crown

DOROTHY MURDOCK KNEW, as a member of the Greatest Generation, that she should be more distraught over the death of Ronald Reagan and she certainly would have been, had the Belmont not been running that same afternoon. Instead of scurrying outside like Marge Burns next door to lower her flag to half-staff, she sat rigid and upright in Fred's old La-Z-Boy recliner, fingers drumming a steady cadence on the armrests and watery eyes aimed like a laser on the television, and worried that the race, only ninety minutes away, would be postponed. She had more of Fred's pension on this one than ever before, and if victory tasted anything like the dry-roasted peanuts she munched, this was her day. So her relief was practically palpable when all they did was flash Reagan's face on the jumbo screen next to the tote board, lower the infield flag, and call for a minute of silence (to which she solemnly complied, and unequivocally would have complied even had she not been alone in the house).

Until Fred died, the most she'd ever bet was a Kennedy half-dollar on the Tuesday morning ladies' league at Holiday Bowl in the summer of 1966, which returned $19.50 at the end of August, ten of which she surreptitiously placed in the offering basket at Sacred Heart the next Sunday, and five of which she slipped with a wink to Jeff, who immediately went out and bought *The Best of Herman's Hermits*. The only other vice she'd had were a couple rum and Cokes and half a Kent cigarette for every three bourbons straight up that Fred drank each night before dinner. She'd hear the station wagon pull into the driveway every evening at 5:20. By then her rollers and hairpins would have been put away in the bottom drawer of the maple vanity, her auburn hair brushed out, housedress straightened, and fresh red lipstick applied. "Yoo-hoo, Dot!" he'd holler as he opened the door. She'd meet him halfway through the kitchen as his greasy hands reached around her for the bar of Lava above the sink. He'd kiss her on the cheek and snap the dish towel playfully at her rear and say, "I guess the Corporation won't float away tonight," or, "An atom bomb couldn't bust the joints I welded today." She'd pinch him just below the belt (unless Jeff or one of the girls was in the room), to which he'd reply with a sly wink and a grin, "Hold the rocks."

The Corporation. That's what everyone called it before it became a national lab. Sandia Corporation employed half the men in Albuquerque, and the pay was good. It was when a man who never graduated from high school could get a decent job as a machinist or plumber, like Fred, or Martin Sedillo across the street, and buy a house on the same block as a physicist or mechanical engineer, like Walt Burns next door. The kids would ride bikes and play basketball and hide-and-seek on summer nights until the sound of somebody's mother screaming her child's name or the piercing whistle of somebody's father would cut through the dark. Games would abruptly end and bikes be dutifully put away, the sounds of a bouncing basketball would fade into the night; doors closed, porch lights were switched off. But the kids grew up, and the sons of mechanical engineers, like Walt and Marge's boys, went to college while the sons of journeymen went to Vietnam. They lost Jeff in 1970. Dorothy never remembered much from that first month, except that a few days after the funeral Patsy Connor from two doors down brought over a Betty Crocker cake, chocolate, and that Marge Burns showed up at the same time, had a piece of the cake, and then said the damnedest thing, something about how her boys would have gladly been there had it not been for the other priorities, and what a shame it was that Jeff hadn't tried to get something stateside, since he was their only son but, thank god, how they still had Kathleen and Emily. Helen Sedillo from across the street said to just ignore her. And then there was Dolores Arroyo, who had lost her own baby years before. She had hardly spoken to Dorothy since then, even though her son had remained Jeff's best friend. The boys had gone to Vietnam at the same time, and Daniel Arroyo was still there. But when Jeff was killed, Dolores never even said she was sorry. All she did was put a mass card in the front door, with a note saying she would let Daniel know.

By that Christmas, Fred's three bourbons had turned to four, with a fifth just before bed, and the lines above Dorothy's upper lip had grown deep and rutted from the Kents she now inhaled all day long. But he still called her Dot, and he still turned red when she brushed her hand over his rear at Corporation picnics; she still freshened her lipstick just before 5:20 each evening, and told the ladies from bowling that theirs was a true love. Kathleen and Emily each earned scholarships to UNM, though Emily was kicked out in her second year and then had too many marriages. But Kathleen gave them three grandchildren, whom they took to Disneyland two summers in a row. And Dorothy and Fred went to Hawaii once after he retired, and then traveled around in a Winnebago until he could no longer pull into the RV parks without scraping the hookups. They learned to play bridge at the senior center in 1997, and then his liver went bad and he died in 1999, just before the millennium. The following September Dorothy met Johnny Davis in the liquor department at Smith's.

Before they ever spoke, she knew by his cart he was a Scotch man and that he liked Fritos. And he pegged her for rum, but he didn't yet know about the Cokes, which were on the next aisle. Then one morning a deep voice smooth like velvet and carried on a scent of Certs and cigarettes murmured from just behind her neck, "Bacardi's on sale, two

fifths for half price at the end of the aisle." She spun around to see the
man who didn't match his voice, short, almost bald, hand extended
toward hers. "Johnny Davis," he said with a grin. They met for lunch at
Denny's a week later, and then he took her to the State Fair racetrack
for cocktails. She put two dollars on a thirty-to-one long shot to win,
because she liked the name of the horse. She bought drinks and hot
dogs with the winnings, and then won a trifecta in the eighth race.
They went again the next week, and she won almost two hundred dollars on the daily double. That's when Johnny leaned into her and said,
"Doll, I know a fellow who can do a lot better by you; he can get you
into any race, any place." He scribbled a name and phone number on
a napkin and said, "Just mention my name." They went together a few
more times, but by then Dorothy had started going to the track alone
during the week. The last time Johnny brought her home he started to
kiss her at the door, just a peck on the cheek, but she held out her hand
and said, "I can't, my heart belongs to Fred," to which Johnny replied,
"Understood, understood." She heard the beep of his car horn as he
pulled away from the curb.

The bookie's name was Mel Wilson, at least that's what was written
on the napkin. "Johnny who? Oh right, Davis, John Davis. Tell him
hello." Mel Wilson was a commercial realtor on the fifth floor of a new
office building downtown. The first thing he noticed about her was the
old housedress. "You'll need a nicer outfit if we're going to do business
in here." The first thing she noticed about him was his enormous belly,
which no monogrammed silk tie, gold cuff links, or Armani suit could
detract from. She opened with a fifty-dollar bet on the third race at
Santa Anita, and bought a turquoise pantsuit and matching sandals
and handbag with the winnings. She began to study the Daily Racing
Form, but continued to place her bets mostly on instinct—a speed rat-
ing and number of starts that combined numerically into her and Fred's
anniversary, or into Jeff's birthday; a filly bred in the same state where
her sister lived; the name of a jockey or a horse. She won more than she
lost, and bought a brown skirt, cream blouse, and black pumps, which

she wore to Mel Wilson's office on alternate weeks until the skirt went threadbare in the spring of 2004.

That May, Dorothy put her money on Smarty Jones to win the Kentucky Derby. He had the name, her favorite brother lived in Pennsylvania and, as Mel Wilson even acknowledged, what a story. The little horse who almost died, the murdered trainer. And it didn't hurt that he was coming off six straight wins. She perched on the edge of the recliner as the race began, and worried the track was muddy. It looked like Lion Heart would take it, when Smarty Jones gradually pulled away with just a furlong to go. Dorothy screamed so loud that Marge Burns called, but she let it go to the machine as she watched Smarty cross the wire almost three lengths ahead of Lion Heart. She called Marge back right away and said something about the roaches being in every drain in the house. She kept her doors and windows closed two weeks later for the Preakness. Lion Heart had the lead again. But just after they entered the stretch, Smarty suddenly fired his engine like a rocket and left the field far behind. As he crossed the finish line nearly twelve lengths ahead of the runner-up, Dorothy jumped so high she fell back into the recliner, spilling the rum and Coke all over the half-finished crossword and onto the carpet which was, fortunately, earth-toned to match the wood paneling she and Fred put in the den when they remodeled back in 1976.

Call it luck, call it fate, or maybe it was just that dreaded week each year when she swam against her greatest sorrow, but Dorothy felt uneasy as the Belmont neared. She found herself worried by all those Smarty parties, all that attention, all those hopes for a Triple Crown pinned on one little colt. Against the odds, Dorothy went with Birdstone to win and even Mel Wilson, whose expression never changed, looked up, raised his bushy eyebrows, and paused just slightly before he took her unusually high bet. But Dorothy had a niece named Marylou, the same name as Birdstone's owner, and Fred's real name was Edward, which seemed close enough to Edgar, the jockey. And their fifty-fifth wedding anniversary would have been earlier that week, right after Emily's birthday, and an elaborate contortion of those numbers resulted in nearly the same figure as a combination of Birdstone's starts, wins, and earnings from the previous season. The signs were all there. So, once the moment of silence was observed and the race began, it came as no surprise to Dorothy that Smarty Jones, pushed into an early lead with a mile still to go, ran out of steam entering the quarter-mile stretch. Birdstone pulled even with just a sixteenth of a mile to run, as Dorothy leapt to her feet and screamed out Fred's name. She collapsed with relief into the recliner as Birdstone took the Belmont by a single length. She drank rum and Cokes well into the night, calculating and then recalculating her winnings. At the track Birdstone, a thirty-six-to-one long shot, returned seventy-four dollars to win. Mel Wilson had given her forty-to-one odds. Johnny Davis had been right.

Around eleven o'clock that night, Dorothy remembered she had not yet lowered her flag to half-staff in honor of President Reagan. She worried what Marge would say behind her back if she didn't (it had taken her three weeks after 9/11 to even get a flag, and Marge, who viewed differences as character flaws, had complained to several neighbors). But, unlike the flag that hung from Marge's pole, or those that soared high above used car lots, Dorothy's was a small Wal-Mart flag on a white plastic stick, which she had affixed to her mailbox with duct tape. There was no half-staff to which it could be lowered. Not wishing the wrath of Marge, she stumbled into the kitchen, dragged a chair down the hall to Jeff's bedroom closet, stood precariously balanced on it, and pulled out the flag that had draped her bullet-riddled boy's coffin at Sacred Heart in the fall of 1970. She went quietly out the door, unfolded it, and shook out the dust. She carefully draped it over the red signal flag on the mailbox, but the weight was too much and the signal flag broke and her boy's flag fell unceremoniously to the ground, tall with weeds and grass not cut since April. Through Marge's open door she could see the glow of the television and the back of her head. Dorothy gathered Jeff's flag into her arms, crossed Marge's meticulously trimmed lawn, and walked slowly toward her porch. Fox News was proclaiming that George W. Bush, like Reagan twenty years before, had come to a cliff above the beaches of Normandy to honor brave boys of the Greatest Generation (as she wrapped herself in a flag from a lost boy of, she thought, some other time). Photographs of Marge and Walt's grandchildren lined the mantle, beaming boys in their Little League uniforms, a girl wearing purple tights and poised on a balance beam, the children for whom her sons had sacrificed so much, she often said proudly. "Well," Dorothy thought but did not shout, as she pulled the flag tight around her shoulders, "my Jeff sacrificed so much that his children were never born." Angry tears boiled up and burst through her clenched eyelids like water through a breached dam. Her head was spinning now, but she backed away, crossed Marge's yard, and fell onto her own unkempt lawn. She sat there for nearly an hour, her back against the old weeping willow Fred swore he would take down after Jeff broke his arm falling from it, until she heard Marge's door close and saw the television and lights go out. She slowly rose to her feet, wrapped Jeff's flag around the streetlight pole, and screamed to no one in particular, "Just wait until your Greatest Husbands' Greatest Livers turn yellow and rot, then see who keeps up with the goddamn lawns!"

Dorothy woke just before dawn, put on her blue robe and straightened her hair in the mirror, went outside with the roll of duct tape and scissors, and attached the small Wal-Mart flag to a lower position on the mailbox post. She carefully unwound Jeff's flag from the streetlight pole, laundered it, and folded it neatly inside Fred's pillowcase. Marge came over late in the morning on the pretense of seeing if Dorothy had heard that a wildfire was nearing the Reagan ranch. She hadn't. As Marge glanced from the open peanut jar on the end table to the empty Bacardi bottle on the kitchen counter, she rambled on about how the ranch house could likely be saved because of fire-retardant gel and some sprinkler system that could soak the buildings and grass. Too bad, they agreed, about the fires in the Rio Grande bosque started every summer by those deranged men left homeless ("by choice," said Marge), supposedly since the eighties. Dorothy flashed on her Emily, a grown woman now, sitting with her bent back against an old river cottonwood.

On Monday, as Ronald Reagan lay in his library, Dorothy put on her faded turquoise pants, a new cream blouse and the black pumps, and went to Mel Wilson's office. He wasn't in, said the receptionist. He wasn't in later that afternoon, either, or the next day, or the next, as flowers and jelly beans and little flags were heaped upon Reagan's star along Hollywood Boulevard. That night she watched his horse-drawn caisson a continent away rolling through the streets of Washington, but all she could think of was Mel Wilson and how much money she was owed and how she was going to find him and how Reagan's casket had been placed slightly crooked on the bier in the Capitol Rotunda, which you could only see from CNN's overhead camera. On Thursday, dressed in a worn, plaid housedress and eyes wild with sleeplessness, Dorothy parked herself on a leather couch in the reception area of Mel Wilson's office and refused to move until she was escorted to the lobby and outside by two security guards. She drank five rum and Cokes and then ran out of Coke and just had rum, until everything went black and her forehead landed on the sticky kitchen table in some untoward baptism by Barcardi. She woke the next day to the sounds of CNN and the middle of Reagan's funeral. She made coffee and then called Mel Wilson's office, but a recording said they were closed that day in honor of President Reagan. Ignoring the heat, she went outside and pulled some weeds and started up the old gas mower. It roared to life in a cloud of thick, black smoke on only the third pull. She started at the sidewalk, maneuvered around the willow and mailbox post, and was halfway through the lawn when she noticed Marge looking out her window disapprovingly. The funeral hadn't yet ended.

Mel Wilson showed up at Dorothy's house in the middle of Reagan's private sunset burial ceremony. He was wearing a wrinkled, green polo shirt and brown slacks, and he handed her an envelope. "Count it." She did and it was all there and he said he'd never before lost his vig, much less been sided, and not to bother coming to the office again. She felt sorry and would have offered to fix him a drink, but he turned and walked away too quickly. She counted the money over and over, caressing each bill slowly between her thumb and index finger, as she sipped her rum and Coke like it was Dom Perignon. By the time she finished, the sunset service was over and she had missed all the speeches, the guns, and the fighter jets, not to mention the kiss.

That night she dreamed the Department of Homeland Security, in honor of President Reagan, stopped the Belmont right before Birdstone crossed the finish line. Four G-men in suits and dark glasses just walked onto the track, raised their right arms rigid toward the sky, and horses and jockeys skidded to a halt, a freeze-frame of flying dust and riding whips suspended in midair. All bets were off. In the dream, the race would be run again that night, but only in front of invited guests and on closed-circuit television. Dorothy decided to try to sneak in and get her money back. After dark, she tied Jeff's Cub Scout neckerchief around her face and crept like a bandit out of the house. She hung close to the hedges to avoid being caught in headlight beams, until she turned the corner where Smith's used to be and found herself on a grassy knoll high above Belmont Park. The track was in total darkness, except for a single horse backlit by a spotlight. It was Smarty Jones, and he was the only horse in the race, except in the dream he was named Smarty Reagan. His jockey looked a lot like George W. Bush, only fat like Mel Wilson. The gun went off and Smarty Reagan trotted out of the starting gate and into the light. Most of the people, having lost all their money that afternoon, were at first silent. Then a few rose to their feet and began to cheer, and then more stood. Marge and Walt were there, chocolate cake smeared on her face, while Dolores Arroyo cradled a dead baby. Smarty Reagan galloped at a leisurely pace down the backstretch, but sped up as individual cheers turned to a collective roar when he turned the corner and headed for home. He crossed the wire to a delirious crescendo, and the crowd threw roses as the track announcer declared him winner of the Triple Crown. As Smarty Reagan took a victory lap, the jumbo screen next to the tote board showed all the news anchors shaking hands and proclaiming he would go down in history as the greatest horse to have ever run.

Dorothy woke in a sweat. The digital clock read 3:20 a.m. She turned on the bedside lamp, and looked around the room. There was her tattered blue robe on the wicker chair in the corner, that photo on the dresser of her and Fred at the luau in Hawaii, Jeff's army picture just to the right, the dog tag that was once draped over the corner of the frame long gone. Her puffy and confused face stared back at her from the mirror above the vanity, as the lace curtain moved gently behind her disheveled, silver hair. She rubbed her eyes, reached across the bed, and smiled with relief at the wad of cash tucked among the folds of Jeff's flag, safe inside Fred's pillowcase. She slowly swung her legs over the side, sat up, and pulled the last Kent from the crumpled pack on the nightstand. She blew a smoke ring on the third try, took a sip from the rum and Coke by the bed, now warm and watered-down from the ice melted hours before, the red smudge from her lipstick clinging to the glass rim like a kiss frozen in time, crushed the cigarette in the ashtray, and turned out the light.

Biography of A Wild Rose

The One Who Stayed Behind

I WAS JUST SIX months old, but that afternoon is vivid with details I could not yet have named. I knew the difference between my mother's and father's voices, though inflection remained visceral. My stomach tightened at raised tones, while my entire head felt warm when sung to. I had no words for the pleasing smell of my grandmother's baking bread, or the scent of wild asparagus carried on the shirt of my favorite brother—only that they floated on the air above my crib every afternoon. And while my intellect had not yet informed me that the cool shade outside the front door was the gift of an old cottonwood, or that the wooden fence surrounding the house was not the edge of the universe, I knew somewhere in my bones I belonged to this place. I knew my home; I knew my name.

"Carmen! Carmen!"

I heard my mother calling me that afternoon. I couldn't see where she was, but her voice was close and loud, and I thought I smelled the perfume she sprayed on her neck and behind her ears every afternoon just before my father came home from work. I had been napping atop a soft, cotton blanket, its fibers familiar with the smells of me, its pink flowers luminous beneath the rays of an August sun that streamed through the west window. Somewhere in the warm, middle distance before senses surrender to sleep, I detected a darkening of the room. A thunderhead had passed between the sun and me. A cool breeze was blowing the lace curtains my grandmother had made; I turned over and buried my head beneath the flowered blanket, and tried to hold on to a few more moments of warmth.

"Carmen!"

There she was again, only by then two of my brothers were in the room. Michael's voice was deepening like my father's, low and soft. And Daniel always smelled of the wild asparagus that grew along the ditch behind our house. A loud clap of thunder rattled the window, and I heard the rain beginning to fall on the roof—big, heavy drops that would either turn into a pounding deluge of water rushing through the rain gutters and splashing onto the wild rose beneath my window, or that would fade away under an emerging sun.

"I think I hear the station wagon!" Michael hollered.

The smell of wild asparagus disappeared into the hallway where Daniel's pace quickened to a run. The rain was beating down now, and the voices of my other brother and sisters had moved from the makeshift swing set outside our back door and into the kitchen, still warm from the oven that baked my grandmother's bread each afternoon. It was cooling on the counter; I thought I could smell its sweetness even from where I lay.

"Carmen..."

The sound of my mother's voice fell away from my ears as she left the room and headed down the hall.

"Miguel!"

She was saying something near the front door, but I couldn't make it out. Someone was cold, and it might have been me. The screen door creaked with the wind, and I heard the heavy footsteps of Michael and my father grow close. Then, as suddenly as it came on, the storm passed. The burst of rain diminished like my mother's voice, and the August afternoon seemed born again as a slight ray of sun made its way past the lace curtains, now just barely aflutter. I imagined the rainbow that had surely risen over the Sandia Mountains, as my father rushed into the room.

I had always loved that time of day—the calm that followed busy mornings of rushed breakfasts, baths, my brothers and sisters fighting over the pink tub as the older ones prepared for school, my mother pushing them out the door, hollering at Daniel to hurry. I loved the quiet that followed the kitchen clattering with dishes set too hard upon the counter, glasses still wet with sticky orange juice plunked in the sink. My mother would feed me, put me in the bath. Then the laundry would begin, the back door would slam over and over as she carried her heavy loads out to the line, two clothespins hanging like cigarettes from the side of her mouth.

My father would have been at work since dawn, his blue jeans covered in sawdust, his shirt reeking with the sweat I would smell as he entered my room each afternoon. I would feel his hands, strong and sure, as he would pick me up and gently pat my back. He'd smile as I opened my eyes, kiss me on the cheek, speak in soft words I didn't yet know. He'd wrap me in the flowered blanket and carry me outside. Together we'd walk the fence line, gaze up into the cottonwood, stop by the wild rose outside my window.

Yes, I had always loved that time of day—the calm that preceded hectic evenings of dinners, more dishes, of seeing that homework was done before noisy play began. I dreamed of the day I could join in that play—Lisa giving me the doll that was handed down to her from Anna, me following Daniel to the ditch and hiding with him among the asparagus ferns, maybe even playing basketball on the concrete court my father poured.

But I was only six months old that day; all I could do was watch. My mother went quiet as she put me down to nap. Perhaps she napped, too, in her bed across the hall. My grandmother moved softly in the kitchen, the sun streamed in through my curtain. I slid slow and sure into my sleep, as I had every afternoon before.

But on that August afternoon the air became suddenly charged, turned electric, as though the storm had been inside the house. The walls seemed to crackle with too much energy; the voices of my mother and Michael were too loud, the footsteps of my father too heavy, too fast. I heard my grandmother call for the others to go outside, the back door slam shut. And then everything went peaceful again. I thought I smelled my father. He was patting my back, picking me up, wrapping me in the flowered blanket, and carrying me down the hall toward the front door. We rushed outside; my mother was lying in the cool grass beneath the cottonwood. Her lips moved, but I couldn't hear what she was saying. Just then the nice woman from next door came in through the gate. My father handed me to her, and the three of us were suddenly in the station wagon. As we rolled out of the driveway, the neighbor held me close, put her soft hand on my neck, my chest, gave me a kiss.

That is what I recall from my oldest memory—more likely some combination of my own senses and family stories I heard over time, gone blurred with the years, like looking back through the plastic my father taped over the windows each winter. It kept us warm, but at the expense of clarity, an accurate view. The nice woman from next door, Helen, has grown old, her children long gone. The twisted cottonwood rises far above the house—taller, thicker. And the irrigation ditch behind the fence runs every summer, its banks still home to a wild asparagus patch. Many have come and gone from the old house. I was thirteen when my family moved away, just a year after Daniel went to some faraway place called Vietnam. I remember worrying he wouldn't be able to find his way home.

The One Who Held Her

SOME BELIEVE THE high, wooden fence that surrounds me is for keeping others out. They are mistaken. It was lovingly raised post by post, rail by rail, picket by picket to form a fleeting sanctuary for those within—a spot of ground that would remember only their footprints, summer shade from a cottonwood whose seed chose only their front yard, a wild rose that seemed to spring from the very foundation of the sturdy walls that kept only their memories, that held only them. Think of my fence as a frame for a painting, or perhaps a photograph, of predictable size but shifting content. It does not serve to keep anyone out, nor does it keep anyone in. There has always been a gate, through which many have come and gone.

I was made in 1949 by the strong, calloused hands of Miguel Arroyo and his three brothers. Within my foundation is a crawl space that brings anyone, sturdy man or small child, to their knees. But who would enter such a space, save the occasional plumber looking for the leak in a copper pipe, an electrician in search of the dangling wire? Above ground I am concrete block, plastered soft brown to appear as of adobe. My floors are sturdy oak—narrow golden strips, quartersawn, showing pith to rind. Rising from them my inner walls—hand-ripping lath, warm plaster. Miguel Arroyo and his brothers rounded my every corner, the doorways to my every room. I have no hard edges (save the exposed block within the crawl space). My ceiling is of thick, heavy beams, tongue and groove, knots peeking like eyes through a stain too dark for Miguel Arroyo's wife. "It's too heavy," she said. "I feel like I can't breathe."

Every square foot of me holds a story, keeps a memory. Miguel Arroyo and his wife had six children. I held all of them, along with a kind grandmother who filled the kitchen with the sweet smell of fresh bread, and with tamales at Christmas. A middle daughter's handprint is set into the concrete of an old basketball court; a beloved cat is buried beneath the mulberry. A boy named Daniel carved his sister's initials into the cottonwood the day before the family went on vacation. Yes, if I could speak, I'd call them all by name. The mirror in my master bathroom has witnessed a father's tears, a mother who one day averted her own eyes and never really looked at herself again—just the daily glance at her hair as she ran a heavy comb through it. An infant gazed up into the cottonwood from the safety of her father's arms, cast her eyes upon each branch, as though she planned for the day she would climb the old tree to its very top, maybe even live there forever.

The One Who Feared Her

I wasn't raised to be unkind, or intolerant. My father worked hard to send us to college; I even considered volunteering for the Peace Corps—going to Africa, or maybe some jungle in South America. I wasn't raised a snob, or some shallow valley girl. But there was something about that house that sent chills up my spine, that caused my shoulders to tighten every time I walked through the front gate. And I was young. Stephen and I were still newlyweds when he got transferred. I had nothing against New Mexico. All I wanted was a place that felt more like home.

Stephen said it had character, culture. Those were the words he used to talk me into moving to Albuquerque's North Valley—not the newer heights, not even the university area—the old, strangely rural North Valley. He said I would feel perfectly comfortable there, that I would fit in just as he and his family had for three decades. But I came from a real valley, the San Fernando Valley. As I said to my friends back home, I'll take an earthquake during rush hour on the Ventura Freeway any day over the dust that blew along the empty ditch behind the house on a March afternoon. Give me the acrid smell of L.A. on a muggy morning over the stink from the horse that was corralled in my neighbor's backyard just two houses down. And let me elbow my way through the holiday crowds along a row of the finest boutiques, where you can find only the newest styles and the best accessories. Give me a Whole Foods just a block away, instead of the neighborhood grocery that smelled of strange ingredients, like menudo and frightening cuts of pork, where the sweaty construction workers and landscapers made a line through the narrow liquor department at five on the dot every evening to buy their bombers, their malt liquor, the miniatures I would find the next day strewn along the sidewalk and gutter on the other side of the fence. Some character, some culture.

The house was a mess when we bought it. Stephen said he would take care of it, that I wouldn't even have to leave my mother's in Woodland Hills until it was all patched and painted, our furniture arranged, the paintings already hung on the walls. He was true to his word. I flew out in April and walked into a clean, fully furnished house, not a moving box in sight. Of course, the yard was becoming an overgrown disaster. There was a twisted old cottonwood right in the middle of the front lawn that looked like it could fall over in a breeze. I wanted to have it removed, but Stephen insisted it was part of the charm of living in the valley. I wondered if he also thought the cotton that blew through the living room every time we opened the front door that spring was charming. And then there was the bamboo all over the place, its runners popping up in the grass and creeping under the buckling walkway. The backyard, on the other hand, was a barren wasteland, save the four beetle-infested elms behind the house that provided shade for various patches of gray and barely green weeds. Stephen said some of it was xeriscape, that we should try and save it. I said it was weeds. In fact, the only spot of color in that entire yard was a single, pink flower on the most ugly, drought-stricken wild rose you could imagine. It was right under the west bedroom window, and was so overgrown and out of control that it was scratching the glass. During a night wind, it sounded like some starving creature was trying to claw its way into the house. It had to go, along with the weeds, all of them.

By far, though, the creepiest thing about the house was the rumbling, cracking noise the heavy wood ceilings made. It sounded just like the Northridge earthquake, especially in the middle of winter nights, and it never ceased to scare the hell out of me. Stephen said it was just a combination of having practically no insulation on the roof, and the wood of the ceilings reacting to the temperature differences between the warmth of the house and the cold outside air. I didn't care; it still gave me a coronary every time I heard it (and the house was never that warm to begin with). In fact, I partly blame that damn noise for the two miscarriages I had in the house—one each winter for the first two years we lived there. My mother said it was just God's way of telling Stephen and me to wait awhile before starting a family. I say it was somebody's way of telling us to first get a better house in a better neighborhood.

When it looked like we were going to be stuck there for a while (and I was pregnant for the third time), I decided to fix up the place, at least as much as that was possible. I was far enough along this time, that Stephen and I figured we could turn the study into the baby's room. We patched the cracks in the plaster that seemed to forever reappear, painted, slapped on some wallpaper with blue bunnies, and started furnishing the room—a rocking chair, a changing table, a mobile that our boy could stare at as he lay safely on his back in the crib. Then I turned to the outside. Stephen and a friend managed to remove the old basketball goal, and made some brick planters atop the concrete. We planted bulbs for color, some perennials, and a few real roses. I got rid of the plants that still looked to me like weeds, and hacked at the roots of that ugly wild rose that kept scratching at the window. We also planted a row of pyracanthas along the entire fence line. The first drunk construction worker who tried to climb the fence would be in for a thorny surprise.

The One Who Found Her

"Oh, and the ceiling makes an incredibly loud cracking noise, but you'll get used to it." With that, the man from whom we bought the house handed me the keys, closed the gate, and drove away with his wife and infant son to their brand-new house in the farthest reaches of the northeast heights.

It was February, cold and nearly dark. I grabbed the lamp from the car, walked back in and plugged it into the first outlet I could find. The light cast a warm glow across the living room and halfway down the hall, reflecting off the freshly polished oak floor and onto the plaster walls. A circle of light from the top of the lampshade made its way onto the dark wood of the ceiling—like a halo—and I instantly felt at home in this empty place.

The movers wouldn't arrive for a few more days, and Paul was working late, so this was my chance to go through each room, to let the floors know the feel of my step, the walls the touch of my hands. This was my chance to know every corner of this place, to absorb its sounds, to fill it with my breath. This would be the repository of memories not yet made, the keeper of secrets not yet told. I stood before the fireplace, the grate still showing the ashes of some other family's warm night, and dreamed of fires not yet set. I walked into the kitchen, opened each drawer, each cabinet. On the insides I could see layers of paint—blues and greens, a hint of a yellow past. How many families, how many layers of paint? It seemed this old house had known the entire spectrum.

On the other side of the kitchen was the hallway that led to each of the bedrooms. I switched on the light in the first room and remembered that we needed to remove the bunny wallpaper that ran in a strip around the perimeter, especially before Jennifer came home for spring break. The bathroom across the hall had a funky pink toilet and tub. The other two rooms were opposite each other at the end of the hall. The one on the east side of the hall was the master bedroom and had a small bath. The one on the west side, though, was long and narrow, as it had once been two rooms, according to the realtor. Some solitary artist had opened it up in the early seventies and turned it into her studio. I walked in, and felt suddenly cold as I tried to determine where the door to that fourth room had been. I opened the closet, but saw nothing, save a few wire hangers left behind by the young father who was probably by now pulling into his new driveway on the other side of town. Just then I heard the ceiling crack. Jesus! He wasn't kidding. It seemed to start in this room, and then rattle and snap down the hall all the way to the front door. I looked up toward the corner, only to notice gaping cracks in the plaster that Paul and I must have missed in our excitement of getting the house. And the room was cold, much colder than the rest of the house. I checked to make sure the window was closed tight, and went back down the hall. We'd get used to it, he said.

I first met our new neighbor, Helen Sedillo, the day the phone company came to install the second line. I had just rounded the house from showing the workman the entrance to the crawl space, when she walked in through the gate bearing a cherry pie in one hand and a vase of flowers in the other. "Welcome to the neighborhood," she said with a smile, "I'm right next door if you need anything." I liked her instantly. She was old and spunky, with a great smile and faded blue eyes that crinkled nearly closed when she laughed. A widow with a sense of humor, and a mind as sharp as the winter sky. "I've lived here forever," she said, as she headed back down the driveway. Just then the workman came around the corner of the house, his overalls covered in cobwebs, his hair lightened by the dust from the crawl space. "All set," he said, as he handed me the work order and a pen. "Quite a little collection you've got down there." Helen turned and gave a half smile.

Spring seemed to arrive early that year, heralded by a dozen robins chasing our old tabby from newly built nests, daffodils and grape hyacinths bursting forth from brick planters, buds showing the promise of pink on an old wild rose beneath the back bedroom window. I removed the row of dead pyracanthas from along the wood fence and transplanted some bamboo in its place. We had the trees pruned—four old elms, a mulberry, the cottonwood in the front yard. I removed the dead branches on the wild rose, fed it along with various perennials that had somehow survived the previous owner. By the end of March, the irrigation ditch behind the house was flowing with an abundant spring runoff that filled the Rio Grande.

"How do you like it so far?" Helen said, as she walked through the gate one Sunday morning. Paul and I were sitting on the porch reading the newspaper. "We love it!" Paul said. Helen followed me into the kitchen and I poured her a cup of coffee. Just as I handed it to her, the ceiling made its cracking noise.

"Well, we love almost everything about it, except for the rocking and rolling of the ceiling," I laughed. "I'm thinking we should give it a name."

Helen replied, "It's Carmen," and smiled the half smile I had learned by then meant she knew more than she said. I almost asked her what she was talking about, but decided against it. It was an old house with old stories, after all, and Helen was an old woman. Instead, I just smiled, and we returned to the porch.

That night I was awakened several times by the cracking of the ceiling. And the east canyon wind didn't help, as the elm seeds were dropping like rain, and the wild rose was scratching against the window in the room across the hall. I made a mental note to trim the culprit branch. As I lay there unable to sleep, I thought of what Helen had said, and suddenly remembered the first time I had seen that half smile. It was when the phone worker emerged from the crawl space, and mentioned having seen something down there.

The next morning I donned my paint jeans, an old sweatshirt, and a baseball cap, and headed straight for the back of the house. I pulled off the rotted plywood cover to the crawl space, stepped down and got onto all fours, as I shone my flashlight through the narrow opening I hoped would accommodate my middle-aged shape. The light revealed a dusty maze of copper water pipes, pier footings, and heating ducts that snaked around and reared up like cobras through the subflooring of each of the rooms. The ground was littered with bits of wire insulation, broken PVC fittings, chunks of concrete block that never made it into the outer walls. There was an old Coke bottle, a barely readable Doublemint gum wrapper. In the middle of it all, about five feet from the entrance, was an empty container of Roundup, clearly flung in there by the previous owner. Nearby was a makeshift marijuana pipe, likely tossed in by some teenage boy as his father came around the corner of the house on a lazy summer night.

As I went deeper into the crawl space, I noticed fewer artifacts of those who had been here before, just brittle leaves in the corners and the occasional bent nail protruding from a dusty grave. But when I turned around, the beam from my flashlight illuminated a small metal box set against the west wall in what I approximated to be the space below the back bedroom window, just inside from where the wild rose grew. As I crawled near, I saw tipped on its side a glass candle with the Virgin of Guadalupe painted on it, the wax halfway gone from some flame long expired, cobwebs filling the empty space. I slowly opened the clasp of the tarnished old box, which revealed a white rosary, a faded swatch of pink, flower-patterned cloth, an army dog tag, and a black-and-white photograph of a handsome man holding an infant in front of a cottonwood that looked very much like my own. After a few moments, I carefully put the photo, the dog tag, and the frayed piece of cloth in my pocket, and promised the creator of this shrine that I would return them. I went immediately next door.

"Helen, can I show you something?" She first held the dog tag, murmured something about a boy across the street. Helen then stared into the photo, gently fingered the cotton swatch, and put her hands to her mouth as her eyes welled up with old tears. I put my hand on her shoulder, as she whispered, "Carmen...."

"She was a beautiful child." And then the words spilled over her lips like a rushing waterfall, splashing on rocks below, spraying in so many directions and baptizing the air between us. A baby girl put down for her afternoon nap, placed with care upon a pink-flowered blanket, beneath it a protective cover for the tiny mattress. Somehow she ends up on her stomach, disturbs the blanket, buries her little face in the mattress cover. Her mother discovers her just as the father comes home from work. She puts the baby on her back; a speck of dried mud is on her forehead. Helen hears a scream through windows left open on a hot August afternoon. She throws the dishcloth onto the counter and runs next door. Carmen's mother is doubled over on the ground beneath the cottonwood, wailing, as her father runs out the front door bearing his baby girl wrapped in the cotton blanket. Miguel Arroyo hands the infant to Helen, and says to get in the car.

"I knew she was gone before the station wagon had even backed out of the driveway. I couldn't feel a pulse in her neck, or a heartbeat in her chest. She was already blue. But I started mouth-to-mouth anyway, just so Mr. Arroyo could hopefully get us safely to the hospital."

I returned the dog tag, photo, and blanket swatch to the metal box below Carmen's bedroom that same afternoon, and cleaned out the trash from under the house. It didn't take much searching through old newspapers at the library to discover that she would have been nearly fifty years old, just a little younger than me, or where her funeral mass was held, and where she was buried. A baby girl whose short time mirrored her own surname—a flash flood of a life flying off the stormy Sandia Mountains on a muggy August afternoon, and rushing through an arroyo on its hurried way to the Rio Grande. A child who stayed behind in the only house she knew, who watched from her perch at the top of the cottonwood as her family packed up and pulled out of the driveway for the last time, and who proceeded to raise herself in the company of strangers.

Her brother returned with Helen a couple months later, and took the metal box and all its contents.

The cottonwood grew a beautiful canopy that summer. On hot afternoons I would rest in the blanket of shade it spread across our lawn, where Carmen's mother once wept. I would peer through the thick branches to its highest reaches and imagine a comforting view—to the east, a rainbow above the pink granite of the Sandias; below, a sturdy house built by a kind father; behind the western fence, a flowing ditch where a beloved brother once played among wild asparagus. My own daughter was home for the summer, her last before her life called her to other places and other people. We picked fresh asparagus from the ditch bank, planted more flowers. And each time the ceiling cracked, I promised Carmen I would visit her grave on her fiftieth birthday, and bring her a single wild rose from our garden.

ACKNOWLEDGMENTS

THERE ARE MANY to whom the author is deeply grateful and whose help in the making of this book was invaluable. Specifically, the author thanks Ladette Randolph, the wonderful, final editor of the entire manuscript. Many thanks also go to Lynn C. Miller for early insight and advice in the structuring and editing of *The River Reader*, and to Rita Talbot, who was the first reader of *The River Flyway* in earlier forms. Other readers included the distinguished editorial board of Arbor Farm Press—Lisa Lenard-Cook, Lynn Miller, Hilda Raz, and Ruth Rudner—along with Sue Hallgarth, Marsha Keener, and friends and fellow writing group members too numerous to mention. The author also thanks Augustine Crespin for his advice regarding Spanish translations unique to the setting, and further thanks those who made the production of this book possible—Mary Bisbee-Beek, Ann Weinstock, David Muench, Sara DeHaan, and Charlie Capek. Finally, a huge debt of gratitude is extended to the publisher, Mary Ellen Capek of Arbor Farm Press, whose unwavering support and determination are forever appreciated.

The author also thanks and acknowledges those literary journals which first published sections of this book: *The River Reader* (excerpt) in *bosque (the magazine)*, "Quartersawn Century" in *Yemassee*, "The Keeper of Mortandad Canyon" in *Hawaii Review*, "My Fifteen Seconds of Flame" in *The Jabberwock Review*, "The Inversion of Jeremy Jones" in *Connecticut Review*, "September Light" in *Bryant Literary Review*, "Texas Armadillo" in *The MacGuffin*, "Where the Dead Man Lives" in *The Pikeville Review*, "Billy and the Butte" (published as "A Backward Walk") in *Oasis*, "My Summer Home" in *Beloit Fiction Journal* (reprinted in *Rosebud*), "The Mayordomo's Son" in *American Literary Review*, "The Great Lunch Debates of 1960" in *Rosebud*, "The Night Smarty Reagan Took the Triple Crown" in *ByLine Magazine*, and "Biography of a Wild Rose" in *Pennsylvania Literary Journal*.

CORRAN HARRINGTON IS a Pushcart Prize nominee, a Santa Fe Writers Project finalist, a Hidden River Arts Eludia Award finalist, a Bosque Fiction Contest finalist, and a New Millennium Writings Award semifinalist whose short fiction (written also as Connie Harrington) has appeared in numerous literary journals. A former lawyer, Harrington also has a background in cultural and linguistic anthropology. She lives in Albuquerque, New Mexico.